The Magician's Trunk

A Sebastian McCabe & Jeff Cody Mystery

ALSO BY DAN ANDRIACCO

The Sebastian McCabe & Jeff Cody Mysteries
No Police Like Holmes
Holmes Sweet Holmes
The 1895 Murder
The Disappearance of Mr. James Phillimore
Rogues Gallery
Bookmarked for Murder
Erin Go Bloody
Queen City Corpse
Death Masque
Too Many Clues
Murderers' Row
No Ghosts Need Apply
The English Garden Mystery
The Woman in Red

The Enoch Hale Trilogy (with Kieran McMullan)
The Amateur Executioner
The Poisoned Penman
The Egyptian Curse

Sherlock Holmes
Baker Street Beat
House of the Doomed
The Sword of Death

School for Sleuths
School for Sleuths
The Medium Is the Murder

The Magician's Trunk

A Sebastian McCabe & Jeff Cody Mystery

Dan Andriacco

Paperback ISBN 978-1-80424-571-2
ePub ISBN 978-1-80424-572-9
PDF ISBN 978-1-80424-573-6

Published by MX Publishing
335 Princess Park Manor, Royal Drive,
London, N11 3GX
www.mxpublishing.com
Cover design by Awan

This one is for
Lois & Michael Bush
friends and fans

CONTENTS

Part One

Part Two

Part One

Chapter One
Magic Unlimited

LESS THAN A WEEK before Halloween, the long-deserted Magic Unlimited shop on Mulberry Street seemed creepy to me in the moonlight, even though it was located just a block down from the mundane Erin public library and Bruce Gordon's flower shop.

Maybe it was those cobwebbed posters of "Houdini, Master of Mystery" and "Thurston the Great Magician" in the front window that had me spooked. Or maybe it was the shop across the street—Mistress Quant's Witch's Brew, a "metaphysical supply store" with crystal skulls and dragons in the window along with its offerings of charms, incense, body oils, tarot cards, and Wiccan and pagan ritual items. This eldritch emporium was next door to the shuttered Looney Ladies Gallery, an art cooperative which didn't survive COVID-19.

Almost as strange as what lay inside Witch's Brew was the presence of the "Quant for Council" poster outside, Zoraida Quant being the owner of the store. City council elections in Erin are held in odd years, which makes them very odd years indeed.

"Do you think most voters know that she's a witch?" I asked Sebastian McCabe, nodding across the street toward the poster as the three of us stood outside the former magic shop.

My rotund brother-in-law shrugged his massive shoulders. "Eccentricity is not a rare characteristic among politicians," he pontificated.

One of the many subjects upon which you are an authority—eccentricity, not politicians.

"Good point," I agreed aloud. One of the other council candidates, Roger Belmont, was running on a platform to ban electric scooters during nighttime hours. To be fair, he was badly injured some months earlier in a scooter-pedestrian collision that put him in St. Hildegard Health for three weeks and left him with a limp.

"Everything is just the way Granddad's left it," explained our companion, looking up at us from working the front door of the shuttered store. "Apparently the rental market is soft, so the owner of the building was in no hurry to get the space vacated." Said companion was beyond pretty, taller-than-me (I'm six-two) and pushing 30 but not hard. Going by the professional name of Alakazandra, Alexandra "Lexi" Pogue should have been dressed like a genie just out of a lamp—not clad in a down jacket with a dunsel cap over her bald head. But I cut her slack for that; it gets cold in Ohio in late October.

"It is fortunate that you have a key," Mac told her.

She smiled pleasantly. "Who said anything about a key?"

Even in the dark of an autumn evening I could see Mac lift an eyebrow. A few moments later Lexi had the door open.

"Welcome to Magic Unlimited," she said, switching on the overhead lights.

That was only the second time I'd been inside the building. Mac had brought me there shortly before his old friend and fellow wizard Septimus Pogue—Lexi's grandfather—closed up the shop and moved into the Elysian Gardens nursing home. To me the place was just a cluttered mess smelling of dust and old paper, with a hint of death thrown in, and nearly as cold as it was outside. But I could see that to Mac the cluttered store evoked something else entirely.

"Ah, the memories," he muttered, stroking his facial forest of graying beard as he looked around. His brown eyes, illuminated by ancient lights that hung from the ceiling, glistened with not-quite-tears. He nodded toward the front of the room. "I performed there under the watchful eye of that devil mask."

Said mask—looking like something out of a bad dream by Dante—was mounted on a wall above a stage at the front of the room, a stage with a dusty maroon skirting trimmed in gold lace. When Mac performed there in the early 1990s as mentor to a group of aspiring young conjurors called the Lords of Legerdemain, two of us had both been students at what was then called St. Benignus College and was now a university where we both worked. Mac, almost three years older than me, had already performed street magic in Europe before he came to Erin for school. After an unfortunate on-campus collision while I was playing with a football and he was flying a kite, we'd bonded over a shared interest in detective fiction—not magic—and then he met my big sister, Kate, known as Kathleen Cody McCabe for many years now.

Dragging myself mentally back from those happy days gone by, I put a supportive arm on Mac's back and glanced around.

The right wall of Magic Unlimited was full of glassed-in bookcases, each packed to the breaking point with everything from pamphlets with a few illusions to great tomes of the prestidigitator's art.

Glass display cases and counters ran the length of the left side of the room in front of the wall, with a space between for the proprietor to stand. Now Lexi was there, where her grandfather had spent so many hours welcoming customers and demonstrating his wares. Zombie balls, Chinese linking rings, coin tricks, multiplying balls, and assorted other staples of stage magic filled the cases. On one of the counters topping the display cases was an old analog cash register. On another lay a rubber chicken.

The shelves behind the cases held what were likely the most expensive illusions—small cabinets, crystal balls, and swords for apparently piercing audience members or assistants.

What I didn't see in my survey of the room was a magician's trunk.

"I thought for sure it would be here, once Aunt Sable suggested it," Lexi said, as though reading my mind. Well, why not? She was a magician, too, like her grandfather and Mac. Too many magicians! "It sat on the stage, like part of an act, for years. But Granddad never took anything out of it while I was around. I thought maybe he moved it here behind the counter."

"On the one hand, I wish you'd thought of the trunk being here earlier, so we didn't have to come out at night," I said. "On the other hand, I wish you hadn't thought of it at all, since it isn't here."

She gave me a frosty look, which with the benefit of hindsight I think I deserved. "Granddad hasn't been in this building for well over a year. It's not like it was top of mind for me."

"Of course not," Mac said, rejoining the 21st century after his mental journey. "This is no time to cavil, Jefferson. That trunk and the letter within are somewhere and we have to find them. I have not yet begun to search."

"There's a back office, of course," Lexi said, "and a storage—"

Just then the front door opened behind us with some force, startling because it was unexpected, the noise followed by a rusty voice unoriginally ordering us to—

"Hold it right there!"

The speaker was a sixty-something woman with short, curly gray hair, large glasses surrounded by blue frames, standing about five-foot-three and chunky. I recognized her from the poster outside as Zoraida Quant, witch and city council candidate.

I also recognized the object in her hand as a gun.

Chapter Two
"Dear Sebastian"

HOW DID WE GET to that point? Let's rewind to the tail end of the previous week—Thursday, October 19, when I got word about the death of 92-year-old Septimus Pogue.

His demise was no surprise, given that he'd been in the last stages of pancreatic cancer. Still, it hit Sebastian McCabe hard. I was just about to assemble my staff for a morning meeting when I received his text message: "I just learned that Septimus died yesterday. Please pray for him."

I told Popcorn, my invaluable assistant director of marketing and communications, to alert the team there would be a slight delay while I made a video call to offer Mac my sympathy. She nodded and told me to give the big guy a virtual hug for her.

"We all have to die, old boy, but I had hoped there would be an exception for Septimus Pogue," was his response to my condolences. Even the lopsided skew to his inevitable bow tie seemed to reflect his sadness, as if tying it that morning was a half-hearted gesture of normalcy. "His body was still warm when the attendant found him dead yesterday afternoon. Alexandra asked me to visit her this evening after working hours."

"Is that the granddaughter you met for the first time at the nursing home some months ago—Lexi Pogue? Also known as Alaka-something?"

"Alakazandra. Indeed, that is the name under which she performs magic for parties, such as the receptions that she arranges in her primary enterprise as a wedding planner. Other than that, I know little about her or her father and aunt, which I rather regret. But I digress. Apparently, in his latter days my old friend gave Alexandra something he wants me to have."

A hat with a rabbit in it, maybe? A woman sawn in half? A floating—

"A letter of some sort," Mac elaborated. "That is, in addition to a magician's trunk that he left me in his will. Alexandra tells me that he wrote the missive to me many years ago and entrusted it to her to be handed over to me upon his demise. However, she herself does not know the nature of the communication inside. Intriguing, is it not?"

I shrugged that off. "The magician's trunk sounds more interesting to me. What's in it?"

"That also is not known, neither to Alexandra nor to me."

"Well, when you do know, let me know."

I was thinking this could be a story for *Ben*, our quarterly alumni magazine ("SBU Professor Receives Magic Legacy"). But the matter soon slipped my mind in the rush of the day's business. Things were hopping in my office as campus life returned to almost normal post-COVID. Not that COVID was really gone more than three years after lockdown—I'd had a mild case the previous month—but masks on students and faculty were few and people no longer uttered the phrase "superspreader event." Six Ohio universities were being sued for a partial refund on tuition by students who contended they received a subpar education during shutdown, but we weren't one of them.

That morning we were more concerned with homecoming, SBU's potential acquisition of a smaller college, and construction of a new building in the Rev. Joseph F. Pirelli School of Arts and Humanities. It was to be named for the recently deceased Ezra Bainbridge.

"Won't the Bainbridge name remind everybody of that whole murder mess a couple of years ago?"[1] asked Riley St. Simon. No flies on her. She and her magenta pigtails, with big glasses the same color, had joined us a couple of years earlier as an intern. Now she handles our very important social media presence on X, the platform formerly known as Twitter, and all the rest of the social media. A drama major at SBU, St. Simon still does an occasional turn in Lyceum Players performances.

"That's inevitable for a while, the dragging up of the whole sordid business every time the Bainbridge name comes up," Popcorn said, punctuating the comment with a chug at her coffee mug. "We just have to suck it up and endure it."

Not that many years back, the St. Benignus marketing and communications operation was just Anneliese Pokorny and me. Now we have St. Simon and Sylvester Link on board—requiring a reconfiguring of our rabbit warren of offices because I discourage them working from home—but I'd still be lost without my bottle-blonde office spouse.

---

[1] See *The English Garden Mystery* (MX Publishing, 2022).

"Look at the bright side," Link said. "At least the murderer wasn't on the faculty—and McCabe, who solved the case, is." That's as close to a joke as Sylvester Link gets. I used to think of him as "Serious Sylvester" back when he was an SBU student reporter more than a decade earlier. Thin, black, and in his early thirties with a small mustache, he still wears his signature khakis and blue sport coat. After getting caught in a round of layoffs at the *St. Louis Post-Dispatch*, he'd returned to SBU as editor and primary writer for *Ben* on a contract basis. He did so well at it that he is now on the payroll.

"There's more positive in the situation than that," I told him. "Ezra Bainbridge was an important member of the Erin community and a long-time SBU board member, as well as the father of a respected faculty member." *Never mind that she was murdered.* "He's well worth the honor of having the building named after him, especially in light of his support for all things Shakespeare in terms of the English faculty and the drama program."

Also, he left SBU a big bequest that paid for the building.

Link wrote it down. "I'll put that in my cover story for *Ben*."

"Let me fine-tune it a bit first. And you can attribute it to G.K." That would be Grant Kingsley, SBU's president. His respect for the importance of communication, coming from his former career as a successful executive, is the reason Popcorn and I now have a staff.

"About homecoming—" Riley St. Simon began.

"FRANK SURE GAVE Mac's friend a good send-off," Lynda observed the next morning while trying to round up our off-spring—Donata, almost 8, and Sam and Jake, just over 5—for the daily chaos that is breakfast time at Chez Cody. "Front page!"

As former news editor of the *Erin Observer & News-Ledger*—"Your Source for Local News," as her coffee mug proclaims—my beloved spouse continues to take a strong interest in the publication even though she's now a stay-at-home novelist of modest success. Frank Woodford, former long-time editor and general manager, now writes a column called "To Be Frank" under the newspaper's new owner, local millionaire Serena Mason. His official title is "editor-at-large," which means he can write about whatever he wants. He knows everybody in town and has played golf with half of them. That gives him plenty of column fodder, having taken up the slack produced when Fred Gaffe was prevented by murder from continuing his "Old Gaffer" column.[2]

Today, "To Be Frank" had moved to page one with the heading **FROM MORTICIAN TO MAGICIAN** and the subhead *Septimus Pogue Lived Full Life, Tutored Aspiring Conjurors*. The accompanying decades-old photo showed the subject looking like the devil in evening dress, what with his pointed black beard and arched eyebrows as he fanned a deck of cards. It was clearly a posed shot from some earlier story. The piece began:

> Septimus Pogue owned a black cat called Houdini. Perhaps Pogue's own greatest escape was the one into a career as the proprietor of a

---

[2] See *No Ghosts Need Apply* (MX Publishing, 2021).

magic shop, mentor to aspiring magicians, and nationally known collector of tricks, books, posters, and memorabilia tied to great performers of the past.

Pogue, 92, died Wednesday at the Elysian Gardens retirement community after a long battle with numerous illnesses, including Parkinson's and pancreatic cancer. He was a well-known figure in Erin, until recently often seen driving around town in a Checker Marathon taxi-cab that he had owned for decades.

"Magic is freedom, because magicians can do anything," he told the *Observer* in a 2001 interview. "That's what's always fascinated me. I saw Harry Blackstone, Sr., saw a woman in half at the Shubert Theater in Cincinnati in 1941. And I thought, 'Wow!' I was 10 years old. After that, I never missed an issue of *Super-Magician Comics*, which featured Blackstone having these adventures all around the world. And I wanted to be a magician myself. But my father told me I had to go to mortuary school as a backup."

The death of his father in 1953 forced Pogue to take over Pogue Funeral Services just as he was preparing to launch a career as a performer on cruise ships, with a signature trick that involved baseball cards where other magicians would use playing cards. Pogue eventually went into partnership with Clayton Belmont and the recently deceased Ira Brown to provide a full range of funeral services in Erin, including cremation. The business continued, despite competition from the Hawes & Holder Funeral Home, until office manager Stephen Collier disappeared in 1989 along with a substantial amount of the company's funds.

"It was disaster, the worst thing anybody could ever go through," Pogue recalled, "but it also liberated me."

The partners sold the goodwill, real estate, and assumed liability of prepaid funerals to Hawes & Holder for a sum that allowed Pogue to open the Magic Unlimited shop at 1323 Mulberry Street. The store, which closed 18 months ago, became well known to magic aficionados in the tristate region. It was also for many years the home of the Lords of Legerdemain, a group of aspiring young magicians Pogue formed and mentored.

"Although I already had some experience as a street magician before I met Septimus Pogue, the hours I spent with him in that shop, along with a group of younger men and women interested in magic, are among the most cherished of my life," said Sebastian McCabe, mystery writer and Lorenzo Smythe professor of English literature at St. Benignus University as well as head of SBU's popular culture program.

"Septimus was a magician of no small merit and could have been a truly great one if his father's death had not forced his life in another direction. We also shared an interest in Sherlock

Holmes, which is not unusual among conjurors. I am truly touched that he bequeathed me his precious magician's trunk, once the property of the Great Blackstone, the very performer who inspired his interest in the thaumaturgical arts."

Asked whether McCabe's mystery novel protagonist, magician-sleuth Damon Devlin, was based on Pogue, McCabe said, "That would be an oversimplification."

"Oversimplification?" Lynda said when she got to that point.

"That's Mac-speak for 'more than I want to admit.'"

"Well, hello, Captain Obvious!"

The column concluded with routine obituary information: Pogue was survived by his son, Adrian; daughter, Sable; and granddaughter, Alexandra. He was preceded in death by his wife, Hope. Funeral services were scheduled for Tuesday—appropriately at the Lyceum Theater, a renovated Odd Fellows Hall on Broadway Street.

"That funeral will be a circus," Lynda said as she dished out oatmeal to the lads and lass.

"No, just magic."

AFTER CHATTING OVER office coffee with Popcorn that morning—defanged for me, high-test for her—I ambled over to Mac's office in Herbert Hall to find out how he was doing and what Septimus Pogue's magical granddaughter had given him at their meeting the night before.

You've heard of the paperless office? Mac hasn't. To call the McCabe office cluttered is like saying the Incredible

Hulk has anger management issues. In the old days, when he used to light the match for his cigar off the "Thank You for Not Breathing While I Smoke" sign on his desk, I used to live in terror that all those stacks of paper would catch fire. Fr. Pirelli, BSU's late president of blessed memory, used to say that there are pilers and filers; Mac is a piler. His piles of books, journals, newspapers, memos, and assorted wood pulp products take up most of the floor space, even though he has ample bookshelves and filing cabinets for any ordinary mortal. That morning my ursine friend stood among those papery piles not practicing some magic trick in honor of his dead friend as I half expected, but doing something far, far worse—playing "Amazing Grace" on his bagpipes.

"Getting ready for the funeral?" I asked.

"The burial, old boy."

Isn't throwing dirt on the body insult enough?

"So, what was in the letter from beyond that Alaka-whozzits gave you?"

"See for yourself."

Mac set the bagpipes back on top of a filing cabinet and by some miracle fished a business-sized envelope out of a sea of white papers on his desk. He handed it to me without further comment. I pulled out a handwritten letter and read:

> Dear Sebastian,
>
> Poof—I'm gone!
>
> I used to end all my emails with that salute to my magical endeavors. If you are reading this, then I really am gone. You well know I don't share your belief that another life awaits us after this one, one of potentially great reward but also

of potentially great punishment in ultimate justice for those who deserve it. On that theological point, for reasons I hope that you will never know, perhaps I am the one who is a wishful thinker.

By this point you may already know that I have willed you my small collection of Sherlock Holmes books and my magician's trunk, a kind of relic which once belonged to the Great Blackstone—Harry Blackstone, Sr. You are also free to retain the contents, although some of them you may want to redirect appropriately.

The most important thing in the trunk is a small fireproof box with a built-in lock that can only be opened by spinning the correct four-digit code. Sherlockian that you are, I'm sure you can figure out the numbers. <u>Do not do so, however, unless I was murdered. Otherwise, destroy the box.</u>

No matter how natural my death seemed, make sure an autopsy is performed. If a request from a relative is required, make Lexi your confidant; she is reliable. In deference to our long-standing friendship, I hope that I can depend upon you to follow these instructions to the letter.

May the good I have done live after me, and the evil be interred with my bones.

      With all good wishes,
      Septimus Pogue

"Murdered!" I said aloud. "Do you think maybe he was just amusing himself to alleviate nursing home boredom? I mean, maybe he didn't really suspect he would be murdered and maybe there's nothing in the box he left you."

Mac shook his massive head. "After more than thirty years of friendship, I cannot credit that Septimus would choose to say farewell in that way."

Neither could I, but I thought it might be nice to not get caught up in a homicide for a change. File that under "wishful thinking." I handed back the letter. "Well, your job is clear, then. You do whatever it takes to get the coroner to perform an autopsy, then you either destroy that box inside the magician's trunk or you open it."

"There is one not-so-slight problem with that, Jefferson. The magician's trunk is missing."

Chapter Three

A Memorable Memorial

"WHAT DO YOU mean 'missing'?"

Mac resisted what must have been a powerful temptation to give me a dictionary definition.

"Although all of Septimus's collections were left intact in his home when he moved to Elysian Gardens, the trunk is not there," he explained.

"Maybe he left it with his son or daughter," I suggested.

"Septimus was alienated from Adrian; they were not on speaking terms. Alexandra called her Aunt Sable, however, and she does not have the trunk, nor could she hazard a guess as to where it might be."

"And it's not at the nursing home?"

Mac looked pained. "I visited him there many times. There was no room in his quarters for an item of such size."

If my genius brother-in-law had thought of the old magic shop then, it would have saved a lot of effort and angst for us and several others. And yet, I suppose the ending of it all would have been the same.

"What's your guess on what's in the trunk?" I asked.

"As Sherlock Holmes said in *The Sign of Four*, 'I never guess. It is a shocking habit—destructive to the logical faculty.'"

An idea hit me like a bad simile.

"Sherlock Holmes! That's probably it, Mac! In that letter your old friend was obviously feeling guilty about something. I'd say he stole some Sherlockian relic, something like the missing first page of *The Hound of the Baskervilles* manuscript or a *Beeton's Christmas Annual*, and he wants you to destroy the evidence of the crime to preserve his reputation."

"But only if he was murdered? That is hardly credible. No, no, Jefferson, that won't do. And even if your fantasy had any shred of credibility at all, Septimus would never wish such a precious item to be destroyed, not even to save his posthumous reputation."

Oh.

"If you say so. Back to the idea of murder, then. Who would want to kill a 92-year-old man with pancreatic cancer, which was bound to kill him sooner rather than later?"

"Most obviously, someone who was about to be cut out of his will and who had access to him at Elysian Gardens."

Obviously.

"In other words," I said, "more than likely his son, daughter, or granddaughter."

"Any speculation along those lines might as well wait until we have confirmation that Septimus was indeed hastened from this vale of tears before his time."

And there the matter sat over the next few days while we were otherwise engaged.

Working through grief, Mac busied himself in part by notifying friends in the world of magic of Pogue's demise. He also asked the county coroner, Dr. Arlene Eppensteiner, to conduct an autopsy. Although Lexi could have made the request as a family member, she asked Mac to do it since Arly is a friend of sorts. Arly agreed in a trice, as Mac might say. A dedicated public servant, she usually appears at every homicide scene even though Ohio law doesn't require it. Like all small-town coroners—and even many big-town coroners— she is stretched because of drug overdoses but has the help of an assistant coroner who is paid per autopsy. But she agreed to move Septimus Pogue to the top of the queue so the body could be present for the fellow wizards expected to attend his memorial service, already scheduled for Tuesday.

Meanwhile, I fielded calls that Friday from *Observer & News-Ledger* education reporter Hadley Reams about the newly announced Ezra Bainbridge Building (he didn't mention the Bainbridge murders, which didn't mean they wouldn't be in his story) and from *The Wall Street Journal* for a bottom-of-page-one feature story on dorm chic inspired by a TikTok craze. I've had worse Fridays.

The next day, Lynda told me she was taking me to Brett McGee's AutoWorks in Cincinnati to buy a car.

"I don't need a new car," I told her. "Not even a used new car. Mine is a classic."

Was that exasperation I saw in her gold-flecked brown eyes? She folded her arms over her more-than-ample bosom. I admired the fit of her ribbed turtleneck, a brown color that nicely offset her honey-blonde curls. Then there was her lovely oval face, her olive skin, her cutely crooked nose, her womanly . . . Frankly, I found it hard to concentrate on what she was saying. Something about—

"—is almost twenty-six years old and it costs about seven hundred dollars every time you take it to Patch Auto Service to get something fixed or replaced."

"Twenty-seven years old, actually. The model year was 1997, but I bought it in 1996. As I said, a classic."

"I would hardly call a New Beetle a classic." She drives a bright yellow Mustang.

"I beg to differ, Lyn—1997 was the first model year. And anyway, what makes you think we have money to throw around on buying a new car, which I will hardly use?" I usually walk or pedal.

Responding nonverbally, Lynda unfolded her arms and handed me a statement of royalties and advances from the publisher of her two family-saga novels, *Bluegrass* and the recently accepted *Ink*. Her business card says, "Lynda Teal Cody, Storyteller."

"I see your point," I said while admiring the number of zeros behind those dollar signs. "Can I at least get a 2010 New Beetle Final Edition?"

"ANY LUCK FINDING the magician's trunk?" Popcorn asked as she handed me my morning decaf and sat in her accustomed spot in front of my desk on Monday morning. At least that hasn't changed with the expansion of our department.

"No, but I now own a new New Beetle. New to me, anyway." It had 69,000 miles on it.

"No!"

I nodded. "I hated to let go of my old New Beetle, but its time had passed."

"Speaking of which, do you think Septimus Pogue was really murdered?"

"Doubtful. From that letter, he seemed to feel guilty about something he did. He was probably being paranoid about it. I don't think the autopsy is going to give Oscar any extra work."

Oscar Hummel, Erin's police chief, is a good friend to Mac and me and a more-than-good-friend to Popcorn (*wink, wink, nudge, nudge*).

"I hope you're right, Boss. What's on the worry list for today?"

THE LYCEUM THEATER is home to the Lyceum Players, an amateur theatrical group of which Sebastian McCabe is a founding member. But on Tuesday, October 24, it was the venue for Septimus Pogue's memorial, with Hawes & Holder in charge. Jonathan Hawes, who played Sherlock Holmes in the Players' production of Mac's play *1895*[3] shortly before our wedding, inherited the operation from his father some years after Pogue & Belmont went out of business.

As I was sitting in the theater with Mac, waiting for the obsequies to commence, the Cody brain ricocheted around several unrelated topics. The Hawes & Holder family business (there was no longer a Holder) somehow made me think of my Grandfather Cody and his brother, Uncle George, who owned the Cody Real Estate brokerage firm together. My father, Samuel Adams Cody, wound up with the business when his cousin Patrick decided he'd rather be an accountant. Patrick took a job with Wells Fargo in San Francisco when I was in high school, thus depriving me of the companionship of my favorite (second) cousin, his daughter Celestina. We'd been very close as kids, Tina and I, while

---

[3] See *The 1895 Murder* (MX Publishing, 2012).

Kate loomed over me as my bossy older sister. Whatever happened to Tina? Asking myself the question made me a little sad as I realized how long it had been since we'd been in touch.

Thoughts of the Pogue family dynamics kicked in then, crowding out the Cody nostalgia, just as Mac leaned over and whispered, "That is Alexandra with her aunt just coming in."

It was the first time I'd seen either one, so far as I could recall. Sable Pogue was in her early fifties, with an athletic body in a pantsuit and with dark hair—somewhere between black and brown—cut short and practical. Her tall, strikingly attractive caftan-clad niece walking arm in arm with her had no hair at all and wasn't hiding it. I wondered whether she shaved her head or perhaps was suffering the effects of chemotherapy. But, of course, I wouldn't ask. Mac answered anyway, in another whisper: "Lexi has alopecia areata." The autoimmune disease, which affects millions of people worldwide, had gained some attention the year before when actor Will Smith slapped comedian Chris Rock at the Oscars after a "joke" about Smith's wife's lack of hair.

Shortly after the Pogue women seated themselves up front, they were joined by a man shorter than either of them, with tousled white hair and wide sideburns who needed a shave. That had to be the deceased's son, Adrian, never mind that he wore jeans and no tie. A few minutes later a plump woman with brunette hair and gray roots sat to his left and grabbed his hand.

As seats filled up with both Erin residents (e.g., Dr. Thomas Abington, Frank Woodford, Lafcadio Figg) and unfamiliar faces—a strong turnout—I looked at the stage. The guest of honor, Septimus Pogue, was there in a pine box that he had made himself and used during his lifetime as the repository for a small but select collection of Sherlock Holmes books and tchotchkes until it was otherwise needed. I knew that from Mac, who inherited said collection. The coffin lay between two folding chairs. I didn't know what was going to happen by way of a memorial, except that Mac said it wouldn't be a traditional religious service. And it certainly wasn't!

"Turn around," Mac whispered. I did so. "Those two men just now entering are Tinker & Skyles."

Not that I needed the identification. The two gray-haired gentlemen were stars of stage, television, and Las Vegas—about as famous a magical duo as Penn & Teller (minus the comedy) or the late Siegfried & Roy (without the lions and tigers). They were a matched set of suave and debonair, today both dressed in dark suits, taking seats in the back row. Just then I heard the sound of a microphone clicking on; all eyes faced front.

"Thank you all for being here." That wasn't a member of the family speaking. Standing on the same stage where Mac had performed as "McCabe the Marvelous, Master of All Mysteries" for a benefit variety show a few years earlier[4] was a man about my age doing a good imitation of Satan, or Septimus Pogue in his younger years, or Damon Devlin. That is to say he was thin, dressed in a tuxedo, and sported a devilish goatee. The distinguished-looking gray at his temples could have been natural or a dramatic touch out of a bottle; the jury was out on that.

---

[4] See "Dead on the Fourth of July" in *Murderers' Row* (MX Publishing, 2020).

"My name is Logan Drake. Septimus's family asked me to be here today." I stole enough of a look at Adrian Pogue's face to know the invitation wasn't unanimous. The Drake name rang a bell with me, but not a loud one. I'll let him introduce himself: "I perform as an illusionist at the Forty Thieves Casino in Cincinnati. That never would have happened if I hadn't been a member of the Lords of Legerdemain as a boy here in Erin. So, I owe my career to Septimus Pogue." A young woman, but not as young as she dressed, came onto the stage in a very stagey way and handed Drake one end of a large red cloth. As he talked, she helped him spread the cloth over the coffin until it covered the latter completely, and then she left.

"Septimus could have been a great magician in his own right if he hadn't pursued a career in the funeral services business, and then later, one as a purveyor of magical marvels who helped aspiring young magicians like me. I'm sure that as a performer he would have amazed us all with such feats as disappearing before our very eyes."

With that, he yanked off the cloth to reveal that the coffin was no longer there on the folding chairs.

At a different time and place, such a reveal would have been met with thunderous applause. In this case, I'm not sure if the stunned silence was respect for the occasion or numbness that someone would do that at a memorial service. I wanted to look at the family but, I have to admit, I couldn't take my eyes off the stage.

"Yes, Septimus is gone," Drake said in a way that struck me as rather sententious. "But he will always be with us in our hearts. In fact, he is here right now in a very real way." Drake spread out his hand toward the—mourners? Or did he think of us as his audience?

Anybody who was expecting something ethereal at that point must have been very disappointed. Instead of ectoplasm or a ghostly presence, the magician's lovely assistant appeared at the back of the theater and walked down the middle aisle with the coffin on those roller things Hawes & Holder uses to move caskets in church funerals.

After that, things got almost normal.

Lexi Pogue left her Alakazandra personality behind—no magic tricks—when she mounted the stage to speak about her grandfather. "He left this world a better place for his being here," she summarized after about fifteen minutes of resumé and remembrances. "That's real magic."

"What did you think about all that?" I asked Mac as we left the auditorium of the theater.

"I suppose they meant well."

I'm pretty sure that's called damning with faint praise.

Next came a crowded reception in the large hall used as a gathering space for selling and consuming refreshments during intermissions when the Lyceum Players have a performance. Mourners mingled and munched elbow to elbow. In the old days—one or two years earlier—such closeness sans masks would have been unthinkable.

Editor-at-large Frank Woodford, a broad-faced black man with more hair on his upper lip than on his head, was busy schmoozing with Rabbi Goldman, a scratch golfer. So, Mac and I gravitated toward the *Observer*'s second-best gossipmonger, news editor Bernard J. Silverstein. Ben would know almost as much gossip as Frank about those assembled, which might include the killer—if killer there were.

"Always a pleasure to see you, Mr. Silverstein," Mac assured him.

The journalist, whose gray hair comes from maturity of years and not from worry, stuck his fingers in his vest pockets and regarded my brother-in-law. "I'm sorry for your loss, Mac. I know you and Septimus were close. May his memory be a blessing."

"Thank you. I am sure he would be pleased by the turnout."

"What do you know about the Pogue family?" I almost said "suspects."

Ben shrugged. "Probably no more than you do. The son, Adrian"—Ben discreetly nodded in the disheveled scion's direction—"is an animal communicator."

"A what?"

"He professes to have the ability to tell pet owners what their animals are thinking," Mac explained.

"Even cats?"

Ben ignored my perfectly reasonable question. "He actually scratches out a living of sorts at it, but not enough to fund some screwy scheme that his father refused to put up the money for, so they had a falling out. His sister, Sable, did well in commercial real estate." He looked around, but apparently didn't see her. "She never married, pinched pennies until Abe Lincoln cried, and retired before she was fifty. Now she's a social media influencer telling others how to do likewise. Apparently, there's a whole movement about that."

"FIRE," I supplied.

Mac arched an eyebrow.

"Financial Independence, Retire Early," I explained. "Those people are even cheaper than I am."

"Truly?" Mac said. "How remarkable!"

Ben went on: "I hear that Sable got along with her father. But wasn't granddaughter Lexi his pride and joy, a chip off the old top hat or something?"

"Quite so," Mac confirmed.

"That's Pogue's old partner over there—Clay Belmont." Ben nodded toward a tallish man walking briskly toward Dr. Abington to shake his hand. Looking good for a specimen in his mid-eighties, Belmont had not-entirely-gray hair, good posture, and a tailored blue suit with bright eyes and tie to match.

"His son Roger operates the local office of the J&J Littlejohn investment firm." Every little town has one of those, usually on Main Street or the equivalent. They don't style themselves wealth advisors. *Au contraire*, as Mac would say, their slogan is "Littlejohn for the Little Guys."

But wait!

"Isn't Roger Belmont the guy who's running for city council on a platform of banning electric scooters after dark?" I asked.

"The very same. I saw him earlier." Ben paused, as if sucking on the pipe that I knew he had in his suit coat pocket. "I don't see him this minute, but he's here. You know, it's a strange coincidence, the third partner in Pogue's old funeral services business died less than a month ago—Ira Brown. He was a member of my synagogue."

"Well, coincidences do happen," Mac assured us. "Although, whether a particular sequence of events is the result of coincidence, divine providence, or human planning is not always transparent. We should speak to the family before we take our leave."

With a bow from Mac and a handshake from me, we moved on from Ben Silberstein to find Lexi Pogue almost backed into a corner by the rather Satanic presence of Logan Drake.

"It's really too early to talk about Granddad's magic collection," she was telling him in a voice that would have kept Winter's ice cream frozen in Barbados in the middle of July. "I'm not even sure the family wants to sell, Mr. Drake."

"Well," he said, "you have my number."

"I certainly do."

To say that the illusionist slunk away like a weasel would be unjust to weasels. Lexi's eyes brightened when they turned to Mac.

"You were one of the few people who visited him at Elysian," she said by way of greeting.

Mac took her hand. "He was a second father to me, Alexandra."

There was a tide of shared emotions here which I could sense but not share in. I felt instead extraneous, out of place, and a bit embarrassed. And then came Mac's old frenemy Lafcadio Figg, intruding on our trio with all the delicacy of a sledgehammer to say, "You have my sympathy, Lexi."

She nodded politely at the short, stocky Figg, he of the gray chin-length hair and mutton-chop whiskers. To give credit where due, Figg was the driving force in creating the Lyceum Players and repurposing the old Odd Fellows Hall as their theater. He did that shortly after retiring as a high school drama teacher in Cincinnati and moving the 40 miles upriver to Erin, almost immediately contributing to his new community. But that doesn't make me like him. He has a long and complicated relationship with Mac, going back decades as fellow Sherlockians. Let's just say that Carnegie Hall isn't big enough for their two egos.

"I didn't know your grandfather well," Figg continued, "but we did, er, share a fascination with—of all things—baseball cards."

"Of all things" indeed! The pompous Figg as a baseball card collector—who would have guessed?

"The difference," he went on, "is that my passion for those ephemeral icons of sports history perdures while Septimus no longer cared. In fact, he once promised to dig out his old cards that he used in his act so many years ago and see whether any of them might be of interest to me. I was wondering if perhaps—"

"That is totally out of place on this sad occasion, Lafcadio," Mac informed him.

"Well, thanks for your opinion, Sebastian," he retorted, "but I'm sure Ms. Pogue can respond for herself."

"I can," she confirmed, "and my response is this: That is totally out of place on this sad occasion." *Neatly done!* As she spoke, I noticed Lexi's wide azure eyes for the first time; they weren't regarding Figg kindly.

"Well," Figg huffed, somehow sounding as if he were the one offended, "perhaps another time."

He turned around, walked a few feet, almost bumped into a dark-suited Roger Belmont, then moved quickly on.

"Ghouls!" Lexi said in Figg's wake, not softly. "Him and Drake both. I'm not giving that one the satisfaction of knowing that I have no idea where Granddad's baseball cards are, or even if he still had them."

Belmont, who wasn't riding an electric scooter, moved closer to us. He stood about five-eight—which made him shorter than Lexi—with neatly trimmed brown hair, glasses, and a square face. Accompanying him was his greying but unbowed father.

"We wanted to express our condolences," said Belmont the younger.

"I'm the last one left now," Clay Belmont said. "That means—"

His son put his hand on the old man's shoulder. "Dad."

"I talk too much, don't I?"

"Thank you for coming," Lexi told Clay before Roger could answer. "Father spoke of you often, Mr. Belmont. Especially in the last few weeks."

"What did he say?" the younger Belmont wanted to know.

"He said Clay Belmont was a survivor."

"Last one left," Clay Belmont repeated with a shake of his head.

"Please let me know if there's anything I can do," his son said, which sounds rote even when not coming from a politician.

As the duo moved on, it impressed me that Pogue's former partner could have appeared in one of those ads for assisted living communities, where everybody looked old but vigorous. In fact, he walked more sure-footedly than his son, the scooter-accident victim.

"WELL, THAT WAS enlightening," I lied as we climbed into Mac's land yacht, a 1959 red Chevy convertible with tail fins about the size of a tiger shark and fuzzy dice hanging from the rear-view mirror. We were to drive to the Ivy Hill Cemetery for the interment. "Have you identified the killer yet, if there is a killer?"

Ignoring me, Mac fired up one of his incredibly expensive Antonio de la Cova cigars. There are few places where he can still smoke other than his own vehicle. I rolled down the passenger-side window in silent protest.

"I shall email Alexandra and warn her to be wary of Lafcadio's avaricious interest in her father's baseball cards," Mac said. "She may not be as aware as we are that baseball cards from the period when Septimus used them in his act, the early 1950s, can be quite valuable."

"Even more so lately," I said. "Sales took a big jump post-COVID, and now with the high inflation rate lots of collectables are soaring in value." Other than that, I know next to nothing about baseball cards or any other collectibles, preferring stock and bond index funds for our Roth IRA and 401Ks. I briefly wondered what Roger Belmont of J&J Littlejohn would advise his clients about collectibles as investments in these high-inflation times. "It couldn't hurt to warn Lexi, but somehow she doesn't strike me as easy to fool."

"I am sure that she is not," Mac said. "Still, my friend Kevin Carter is a serious collector and could advise me on the current values of vintage baseball cards, which might be helpful."

"Is he a magician, a Sherlockian, or a mystery writer?"

"A Sherlockian mystery writer who dabbles in magic."

"Of course." *Why did I ask?*

Cigar in mouth, Mac was just about to turn the ignition key when we heard the ping of his cell phone. He pulled it out of his pocket and looked at the incoming text message.

"This is from Dr. Eppensteiner," he announced. "She was kind enough to let me know the preliminary results of the postmortem. Although it will not be official until she completes the written report in a few days, she is confident that Septimus was poisoned with fentanyl."

Chapter Four
Off the Record

"I CAN'T BELIEVE It," Oscar Hummel said.

"Believe it," I told him.

On the morning after the funeral, we were sitting in the Chief's office at the police station, an Art Deco former bank building on Court Street, discussing the coroner's preliminary results. Not that it was news to Oscar, I bet. I'm pretty sure Popcorn told him about two minutes after I told her, and he'd been stewing ever since about Arly not telling him herself. (Got that?) But she's an elected county official, Oscar is an employee of the city of Erin, and her findings weren't yet official. I figured she only told Mac as a courtesy in his role as a representative of the family who had asked for the autopsy on their behalf. Or maybe it was because she wanted to give him a running start on the case, knowing that wild dinosaurs couldn't keep him away from it.

"Fentanyl as the murder weapon is not much of a clue to the killer, is it?" Mac observed, unhelpfully.

"Considering that it's a major cause of drug overdose deaths and rural Ohio is especially hard hit, I'd say not," Oscar agreed sourly. "The stuff is all over the place illegally, sometimes combined with animal tranquilizer—'tranq' in street talk—to ramp up profits for the dealers. Plus, it can be legitimately prescribed for extreme pain. The real trick would be getting it into the victim."

"Not really," I said. "The killer could have given it to Septimus in a pill. They must be dispensing pills constantly at Elysian Gardens."

"Or the miscreant could have injected it into his intravenous line," Mac added. "Either way, he or she had to be on the scene. There are only three possible ways for that to happen—the killer was either an employee, or a visitor who signed the register at the front desk, or someone who managed to enter by some subterfuge."

"Wait a minute!" Oscar sat up. "How do we know Pogue wasn't prescribed the stuff and got an overdose—a huge screw-up?"

"Because Dr. Eppensteiner said so, and we can trust her. She is highly proficient, as I am sure you will acknowledge. Although she did not say so in our brief exchange, I presume she had access to Septimus's medical records and could ascertain that he was not prescribed the opioid. Either that or the amount of fentanyl in his body ruled out an accident."

"I'll have my crack troops check the sign-in sheet to see who visited Pogue," the Chief hurried on, "and the employee roster to see if any names ring a bell."

Oscar is a couple of years younger than his lady friend (my label) Popcorn, with sixty extra pounds in his lap and a balding noggin almost always covered—today by his official police headgear. He looked in desperate need of a cigarette as we discussed Erin's latest homicide. He'd transitioned to vaping a few years back, but even that was banned in most places and just this month *The Cincinnati Enquirer* had run two front-page articles on the dangers of the practice. So, our top cop settled instead for pouring himself a cup of coffee, black. Mac followed suit, using the **I REFUSE TO ACT MY AGE** mug that Oscar kept for him next to the Keurig machine.

After his first long sip of the caffeine-laced brew, Oscar exploded with: "Hell's bells! It gives me the creeps to think that Mom was in a rehab unit there at Elysian during COVID. Some whack job could have killed her." I doubted that. Alma Hummel is older than Septimus Pogue and apparently immortal. She lives with Oscar and acts like he lives with her, which is why wedding bells are not in his foreseeable future. "Why would anybody murder a 92-year-old man anyway?"

"Obviously to stop him from changing his will," I said.

"Or from doing something else," Mac added.

"Eh?"

"The will scenario is only one possibility, Jefferson. An elderly man is capable of any number of actions that someone might have wanted to prevent—telling someone else's guilty secret, for example."

You didn't say that yesterday!

"That narrows the field of suspects all the way down to everybody," Oscar said, "because everybody has something to hide."

"What's your secret?" I wondered.

He ignored me, changing the subject. "I don't like any of that stage magic mumbo jumbo. And this case is going to be filled with magicians, isn't it?"

"Several, possibly," Mac conceded. "And also, a magician's trunk, which is currently missing and may or may not have anything to do with the murder."

He expounded upon that, filling Oscar in on Lexi's inability to find said trunk.

"Well, see, you're already involved," the Chief said at the end. "That being the case, maybe you could poke around a bit, ask a few questions informally, since you're a friend of the family. You'd have an in, and I'm sure your relationship with the Pogues wouldn't cloud your judgement if one of them is the bad guy."

That was laying it on pretty thick. Oscar's attempt to ask for help without asking for help was embarrassingly transparent. On occasion he has referred to Mac and me as consultants or unofficial deputies, but the last time murder disturbed his nap he was convinced that the combined forces of his officers (Gibbons, Lehmann, Mentzel, Bertsch, *et al.*) and the St. Benignus University Police could establish the killer without us. That didn't end well for Oscar.[5] Now he was trying to bring us in without admitting that he'd overestimated the power of police routine in that business and that he was afraid the situation might be similar in this one.

"And I am not sure that I—"

I don't know what Mac wasn't sure about, because at that moment Oscar's office door opened and his perky executive assistant Holly Burdette stuck her head in. "Visitor, Chief!" Holly is under 30 and looks even younger, with pixie-cut hair and boyish figure, but holds degrees in business and criminal justice. In just a few years she'd become invaluable to the small police department.

Oscar scowled, which his broad face seemed made for. "You know we're having a meeting."

---

[5] See *The Woman in Red* (MX Publishing, 2023).

"Of course you are," said the visitor on her way into the room—a tall (six feet before the three-inch heels), slim woman with straight, straw-colored hair beneath a jaunty black beret, her long legs well hidden at the moment by a belted trench coat. "A meeting with Sebastian McCabe. What else would you be doing after learning that an elderly citizen has been murdered in a nursing home? Especially when he was a friend of Mac's."

"So young and yet so cynical!" I tutted.

"Hi, Jeff."

Johanna "Tall" Rawls is the workhorse of the *Erin Observer and News-Ledger*'s small reportorial staff. Lynda hired her a dozen years earlier and the two have always been close. They confab frequently even though Lynda is now officially out of the newspaper game (though her heart isn't).

"Murder?" Oscar bluffed. "What do you know about a murder, Rawls?"

"I know that Dr. Eppensteiner conducted an autopsy on Septimus Pogue at the request of the family, funneled through Mac here, and her unofficial finding is that Pogue was poisoned."

"Where did you hear all that?"

"I can't reveal my sources."

"It must be admitted that you have good ones," Mac said.

Oscar glared at him, no doubt wondering *why* that must be admitted. I was glad the Chief was looking at Mac and not at me, because right then I realized I may have mentioned something to Lynda about the autopsy in an unguarded (perhaps even marital) moment, and she may have—

"So, anyway," Johanna said, "what's the status of the investigation, Chief? Off the record."

"There is none."

"Tell me another. You guys aren't talking football. Mac wouldn't know the shape of the ball."

"A slight exaggeration," Mac rumbled.

Very slight.

Oscar sighed. "You and I have known each other too long to play games, Rawls. We've always been straight with each other, right?"

Tall Rawls considered. "More or less," she conceded.

"Right. So, I'm not yanking your chain here. I haven't received an official report yet, therefore I haven't launched an official investigation."

Mac would have said "ergo," not "therefore."

"I presume the key words are 'official' and 'yet,'" Tall Rawls volleyed back. "Arly wouldn't confirm the autopsy to me, much less her findings, which means she hasn't written the report yet. I asked her to let me know when she does. She didn't say she will, because that would confirm there was an autopsy, but she will."

That impressed Mac. "Your excellent reportorial skills are worthy of a larger media market," he observed.

She sighed. "I've been thinking about that a lot lately. But the only newspapers in larger markets that aren't laying off reporters are the ones that are shutting down."

"Seth wouldn't want to leave town anyway," I observed. Her boyfriend's family is Amish, and distance from them would be a problem for him.

Reddening slightly, which was cute, Tall Rawls turned to Mac. "About the murder—"

"If there is one," he said.

"—what's your first step? Just between us chickens. I promise I won't write a word—or at least I won't turn it in to my editor—until the autopsy is released."

Mac chugged caffeine while he thought about that. Then he said, "A visit to my old friend's granddaughter would seem in order."

Chapter Five
Pogue Family Values

LEXI POGUE WAS in the middle of planning a wedding when we caught up to her that afternoon after I knocked off work for the day (not that a vice president of marketing and communications is ever off the clock). She worked out of a tidy paperless office (!) in her home, in a modest A-frame house surrounded by woods just within the Erin city limits.

She answered the door with a phone to her ear. "That won't be a concern, I assure you," she was telling the person on the other end. She held up a finger in the universal "wait a minute" gesture, closed the door, and reopened it three minutes later with a black cat in her arms. Being an assistant sleuth, I deduced that this was her grandfather's pet, Houdini, about whom Frank Woodford had written. "Sorry about that—nervous mother of the bride for a wedding I'm planning," she explained. "The ceremony is on Halloween and I'm performing my special wedding magic act as well."

"During the ceremony or at the reception?" I asked, thinking I was joking.

"The reception—this time. But sometimes I preside over the ceremony. I do bar mitzvahs, too, but just the reception."

I'll keep that in mind.

She led us into the house, an open floor plan with a living room area on the left and dining on the right. The dining area was set up as a home office, which made me a little envious. My laptop is set up on our screened-in porch.

We seated ourselves in a cluster of three living-room chairs. If there were any vanishing coffins lying around, or top hats suitable for producing rabbits, I didn't notice.

"Do you plan many weddings, Alexandra?" Mac wondered. "The institution seems rather out of favor in this benighted age."

"I know what you mean. My boyfriend, Jack, is slow to commit, unfortunately." Her smile was strained. "But I have clients walking down the aisle—when there is an aisle—almost every week now that we're back from COVID. With that and the magic gigs, I do all right financially."

Translation: I don't need my grandfather's money.

"Actually, the work is good for me right now, despite having to deal with mothers of the bride," she added with a theatrical shudder. I suddenly had a flashback to my own wedding and the horrifying antics of Lynda's famous actress mother, but I shoved that train wreck back into the farthest reaches of my subconscious (until now) and tuned back into Lexi: "Being busy takes my mind off being angry about Granddad. It's just not right that he spent all that time in the nursing home, with the cancer and Parkinson's and a laundry list of other ailments, taking like twenty pills a day, and then some asshole murdered him. And how could that even happen with all the people that are around at Elysian Gardens?"

Mac didn't bother to pick nits by pointing out that Arly's finding of homicide was unofficial. He did, however, take her question to be information-seeking rather than rhetorical. He replied:

"The exact method is unknown. What we can say for certain, as I mentioned in our phone conversation, is that he was poisoned by fentanyl."

"That just adds to the weirdness. Fentanyl in a nursing home?"

"It is not only used for illicit purposes, although one hopes that today it is prescribed by physicians only with great caution. Have you informed your father and your aunt of the situation?"

She nodded.

"And their reaction?"

"Dad said, 'Are you kidding?' I'm like, 'Who the hell would kid about a thing like that?'" She sighed. "Maybe I'm being too hard on him. He must be feeling pretty bad that he and Granddad hardly spoke, and Dad never even visited him at Elysian."

"I understand they had a rift over some sort of investment scheme that Septimus considered unwise," Mac said.

"Right. Because Dad is a nutball."

There's a lot of that going around.

"Would you care to explain?"

Lexi stroked the cat on her lap. It may have been just a nervous gesture, but the cat seemed to appreciate it. "Dad got furious because Granddad refused to loan him money to start a franchise network of animal channelers with a 1-888 number. You know he communicates with animals, right?—tells their owners what they're thinking in return for a fee of sixty-five bucks for a 30-minute session, usually by phone?"

That's 130 bucks an hour! I'm not sure Adrian Pogue is the crazy one in that transaction.

"I have heard something of the sort," Mac acknowledged.

I wondered what Houdini (the cat, not the escape artist) thought about animal channeling, and then I thought that Adrian Pogue supposedly could tell me what he thought about it, and then I thought that I was thinking too much.

"Nothing ever came of 1-888-DOGTALK or whatever," Lexi continued, "but now Dad has this crackbrain idea of starting an animal B&B. He says a lot of his clients ask for that, especially the dogs. He considers the animals to be his real clients."

Meanwhile, back on Planet Earth—

"And your Aunt Sable's reaction to the postmortem news?"

"At first, she sobbed and cussed, then she was kind of like, 'I told you so.' She visited Granddad a lot, and she's been worried for a long time that he wasn't getting the best care in that place, or even worse."

Suddenly, I had visions of Donald Harvey, who claimed to have killed 87 patients in hospitals he worked at as an orderly in Ohio and Kentucky in the 1980s, although official estimates put the number at a mere 37 to 57. Mac's thoughts were closer to home.

"Do you know the provisions of the will?"

"Sure. I'm the executor."

A McCabe eyebrow shot up. "Why you?"

"Granddad asked me to do it when he re-wrote the will after the falling out with Dad. Aunt Sable wasn't interested."

"And the provisions?"

"You know most of it: I get Houdini, Granddad's magic collection that he kept in a special room in his house, and that antique Checker cab he was so proud of. You get the trunk with its contents and the Sherlock Holmes books and doodads he kept in the coffin. The rest is split between Dad and Aunt Sable, including the contents of the house and the proceeds from its eventual sale."

"Septimus did not disinherit your father, then?"

"To spite him from beyond the grave? You know Granddad wasn't like that, Mac."

"Certainly, I would not have expected such an action from Septimus. However, sometimes people surprise us. And along that line, did you have any indication that he planned to alter his will?"

She crunched up her face in a question mark. "Not at all. Why do you ask that?"

"I ask many things. In my experience, that is an excellent way to get answers—although not always true ones."

"Am I, like, a suspect?"

"You would be if this were a detective story," I said, just to keep my hand in. "But you'd be innocent."

"THAT WHOLE SUSPECTING the nursing home staff thing has me thinking," I said back in the Macmobile. "Donald Harvey killed all his victims by smothering them with pillows. Why didn't the killer do that to Septimus instead of fooling with the drug? The old man would have been too weak to resist, wouldn't he?"

The cigar almost fell out of Mac's mouth. "By thunder, Jefferson, I believe you are on to something. Bravo! Let us think about that. We could speculate that the killer feared he or she would not have the intestinal fortitude to hold down the pillow for the length of time required, as opposed to injecting the fentanyl and walking away." He shook his melonic head. "Possible, but hardly plausible. There is most likely another reason."

I made a mental note of that.

Sable Pogue lived just a few streets over from the Cody bungalow on Campion Lane.

"Lexi warned me you were coming," was the way she greeted us at the door.

"I trust our visit will not be painful," Mac said.

"Yes, it will." She said it matter-of-factly, not picking a fight. "I hate to think about how my father spent his last days."

Her house was a one-story, white brick with columns in front—pleasant enough, but not what most people would have expected from someone who made enough money in commercial real estate sales to retire in her forties. But then, we knew from Ben Silverstein that she was part of the FIRE movement, which is all about living frugally, saving a lot, and keeping a big cash balance for emergencies. Those are all good things, but some of the FIRE advocates I've read about are a bit extreme even by my standards—and I've been known to run water through the same coffee grounds twice to save money. I wondered whether Sable cut her short, dark hair herself, considering what Lynda pays Myrtle White at the Glam Gurlz beauty salon every month. (But worth it!)

Sable had us join her in the breakfast room, which had a nice view of an ample backyard with nice landscaping and a small fountain.

"I take it that you visited your father often at Elysian Gardens," Mac said by way of opening.

"Lexi and I both did, but not my worthless brother. In fact, I visited Dad on Wednesday, the day he died. If only I'd known . . . " She swallowed.

"We understand from your niece that you feared Septimus was being mistreated."

"Not feared—I knew he was."

"Mistreated in what way?"

"Through neglect and even abuse. I overheard one of the employees, a man named John Rentz, taunt him about his inability to perform magic because of his Parkinson's. 'No more "hands quicker than the eye," old man.' That's what he said, the bastard. That was just cruel. I reported him to the management and all I got was an assurance that he would be reprimanded. Reprimanded! And now my father is dead. I had a plan: I was going to put a video camera hidden inside an alarm clock on the dresser across from Dad's bed. The one I found on Amazon records 24/7 in five-minute increments on a memory card and holds hundreds of hours. I got the idea from the security cameras outside Elysian."

"An excellent idea!" Mac said.

"Oh, yeah, brilliant," Sable said bitterly. "Except that the camera arrived on my back porch the day he died. Fat lot of good it did then." She paused. "I can't stop thinking about the sad shape he was in the last time I saw him. I'm not sure how long he would have lived anyway. He'd been fighting pancreatic cancer for years, but he knew the fight was about over. Dr. Abington suggested hospice care, and Lexi and I were working ourselves up to talking to Dad about it. But to rob him of whatever life he had left, and however sad it was—"

She trailed off.

Some people might call that putting him out of his misery. Not me, but maybe somebody with access to fentanyl.

"Who do you think killed your father?" I asked.

Sable looked at us like we had multiple heads, and all of them empty. "Isn't it obvious?" She downed tea. "It must have been that monster John Rentz getting back at me."

"He certainly did not want for means or opportunity," Mac said. "Still, that does seem a rather drastic response to a reprimand." He moved on. "There is another puzzle, hardly in the same league as Septimus's death but vexing, nonetheless. Do you have any idea what happened to the trunk your father owned which once belonged to Harry Blackstone, Sr.?"

"I know exactly where it is."

"What!" That was my interjection.

"It's in the old shop, Magic Unlimited. I saw it there about a week ago when Dad asked me to bring him one of his posters to decorate the wall of his room—'Blackstone, the World's Master Magician.' It was always one of his favorites."

"The shop!" Mac boomed. "Of course! Why did I not think of that before?"

"Lexi and I didn't either," I pointed out. That didn't seem to help. "It hasn't been open for ages."

"The lease doesn't expire until next year and Dad couldn't bring himself to have us clean out the inventory."

"We must go there without delay." Mac stood up.

"Lexi will get you in," Sable said. "Call and ask her to meet you there."

As a parting shot, I told Sable I was going to check out her FIRE blog. She gave me the web address.

"What are your thoughts on crypto?" I wondered, only out of curiosity. I don't do cryptocurrency—or casinos.

She didn't need to ponder her answer. "Stay the hell away from it! I took a flyer in that stuff early last year on my financial advisor's advice. He was big into it. Good thing I only risked a little of my stash, because I lost most of what I put up. That wasn't fun."

No surprise there. Crypto was in the toilet of late, highlighted by the bankruptcy of FTX cryptocurrency exchange and the arrest of its founder, Sam Bankman-Fried, on fraud and other charges. He was on trial as we spoke and was convicted early the following month. The year before, when Lynda and I hosted a party for that Super Bowl with the Cincinnati Bengals, TV coverage of the game was packed with $70 million worth of commercials featuring A-list stars and athletes hawking crypto. In the roughly 20 months since, a number of those crypto hawkers had wound up paying fines to the Securities and Exchange Commission—which was better than the prison sentences facing several crypto executives.

I was about to ask Sable for her take on index funds when the doorbell rang. She looked at her phone. I made a mental note to investigate installing Ring at Chez Cody. Burglaries as well as homicides had exploded everywhere since the pandemic, not just in Chicago, LA, and New York.

"Oh, fiddlesticks." Actually, the influencer said a shorter word than that. With a sigh, she went to the front door and yanked it open.

"Can I come in?" This opening salvo from the disheveled Adrian Pogue wasn't the warmest of brotherly greetings, but his sister didn't seem to expect anything more.

"Join the party," she told him. Which was good because he was already walking through the door.

By this time, Mac and I had entered the small hallway with the intention of leaving.

"I know who you are," Pogue told Mac accusingly. "You're that McCabe guy who was a friend of Dad's—the one who's always sticking his nose into police business."

Fair description.

Mac gave a brief bow. "My pleasure, Mr. Pogue."

"The pleasure is all yours."

Not very original.

"I'm Jeff Cody," I offered.

Pogue turned to his sister. "Lexi called a few minutes ago and said the old man was murdered. She wanted me to know before it became official, but it sounded like telling me was an after-thought. Even worse, she wouldn't let me talk to Houdini. He must be a basket case. Did you know this?"

Sable glared. "About Dad's murder or about his cat's emotional condition? If you mean about Dad, yes."

"Why didn't you tell me?"

"I didn't know you'd be interested." It would have taken a mop to clean up the sarcasm that dripped from Sable Pogue. Her brother changed his angle of attack.

"It's your fault."

"My fault!"

"You and Lexi. You were the ones who visited Pop at that nursing home all the time. How could someone kill him?"

"One of us was there almost every day, but not all day. You were never there at all, you waste of Pogue DNA!"

It was hard to read the look on Adrian's unshaven face, but "chastened" wasn't it.

"Our last visit didn't go well," he mumbled. "Pop completely underrated the profit potential of animal B&Bs. But he was still my father. And I'll tell you this, Sable." His voice rose. "I'm going to light a fire under Oscar Hummel to make sure that finding Pop's killer is the number one priority of the Erin Police Department."

"Jefferson and I hope to be of some assistance in that regard," Mac intruded.

Pogue gave him an "are you still here?" stare.

"Any ideas so far?" Sable asked—a sincere question and not sarcasm.

"Just one: I cannot rid myself of the feeling that the magician's trunk is somehow the key to the matter. I appreciate your telling us its location."

And that's how instead of being home on Campion Lane that October night with Lynda and my three by-now-sleeping offspring, I was at a deserted and creepy magic shop with a witch pointing a gun at me and my two companions.

Chapter Six
Witching Hour

THE GUN WAS a Sig Sauer P365, Mac informed me later. I had no idea whether Zoraida Quant knew how to use it, but it occurred to me that she was probably more dangerous to us if she didn't.

"Please put down that weapon, madam," Mac said.

"Not until I call the cops."

"Oh, for crap's sake," Lexi exploded. "I'm Lexi Pogue. My grandfather owned this store. Want to see my driver's license?"

"No, just take your hat off."

Lexi did so.

"Okay. I recognize your bald head." Quant put the gun into the folds of her midnight blue dress, which I have to admit played nicely off her curly gray hair. "I saw you stop by here with Pogue one day last summer."

Nosey witch.

"That's right," Lexi said. "He begged me to bring him by, said it might be one last time, which it was."

"I'm sorry for your loss." The statement sounded rote, as it usually does. "Your grandfather was an okay guy, I guess, but in playing the magician he mocked the elemental forces that he pretended to summon—never a good idea. Maybe that's why he's dead."

Before Lexi could offer her opinion on that—which, judging by the look on her face would have been incendiary—Mac said:

"I beg to differ."

Mainly because elemental forces don't use poison.

The witch gave him a closer look. "You're Sebastian McCabe," she said. "I once saw you name a murderer on live television. I'll never forget that."[6]

"Nor shall I, Ms. Quant, I assure you. Approaching us bearing arms was a rather decisive action on your part. What made you assume we were burglars rather than relatives of the recently deceased owner of this establishment, or perhaps representatives of the owner, Mr. Mackie?" That would be Gulliver Mackie, "wealth manager" to the hoi polloi, major landlord in downtown Erin, and spouse of my immediate boss at SBU, the redoubtable Lesley Saylor-Mackie.

"Because this wasn't the first time I've seen suspicious activity around here. Last Thursday night I noticed the light was on. I kept an eye on the place for a while, but then I had to run a private crystals class for two. By the time we finished, the light was out."

"Crystals class?" Lexi asked.

"You know—grid work, body layouts, crystal identification, the seven chakras."

Oh, that.

Quant had nothing more to offer except a "Quant for Council" campaign flyer with a bewitching photo of her and

---

[6] See *Bookmarked for Murder* (MX Publishing, 2015).

the slogan, PUT SOME CHARM INTO CITY COUNCIL, which played off of one of her main product lines.

When she'd gone, Mac put the obvious into words: "Someone stole the trunk, most likely by forced entry."

It didn't take long to confirm that last part. A window had been smashed in at the back door, allowing the intruder to reach a hand in and unlock it from the inside.

Lexi said a word that used to be unprintable. "I told Aunt Sable we needed an alarm even though the business is closed. She didn't want to spend Granddad's money on it."

"So, the killer has the trunk, and whatever Pogue left for you inside," I told Mac.

"Perhaps, Jefferson. And perhaps not. By Thursday evening the news of Septimus's death had become widely known to his friends and acquaintances, quickly spread through social media. The thief could have been a collector of magic memorabilia who theorized that something especially significant was inside—a hitherto unknown Blackstone relic, for example. That would have been appropriate, given the origins of the trunk."

"Logan Drake is a collector," Lexi said. "You heard him trying to get his grubby paws on some of Granddad's stuff at the reception after the memorial. I'm sorry I ever asked him to be part of that day."

Mac stroked his hairy phiz. "I knew Mr. Drake briefly and not very well many years ago, when he was a member of the Lords of Legerdemain. He performs in Cincinnati, so he cannot live far away. The magical duo of Tinker & Skyles, on the other hand, are famous denizens of Las Vegas. One would have to posit that they knew of the speculated rare treasure and came here to steal it, somehow knowing that

Septimus had closed his shop but not disposed of the contents. Preposterous!"

Said the man who writes "impossible crime" mystery novels about a magician.

"They would have simply waited for him to die, and then bought what they wanted," he rolled on. "They are not paupers."

"If I do sell," Lexi said, "it will be to them or to somebody who's not Logan Drake. But that won't be anytime soon."

"As to the thought that Tinker & Skyles would have killed Septimus to attain some magic memorabilia," Mac piled on, "that is even more beyond the pale. Not to mention the fact that they would somehow have had to get into Elysian Gardens, where they did not sign the visitor register."

"We're talking about collectors here, Mac," I pointed out. "And magicians. The first means they'll do anything, and the second means they *can* do anything."

"Valid points, old boy, to be sure. I suppose we should ask Oscar to have one of Erin's Finest check their alibis."

"We should. On the other hand, though, the magic wasn't Pogue's only collection, and his fellow wizards aren't the only ones who wanted to get their hands on something of his." *I was on fire!*

"You refer, of course, to Lafcadio."

"Figg!" Lexi said. "He was the other one, besides Drake, who couldn't even wait until after the burial to try to get his hands on something that was Granddad's. In his case, his old baseball cards. You warned me that they might be valuable, Mac, but I don't know where they are. They could be in the trunk, for all I know, in which case they belong to you."

"As attractive as I find the idea of Lafcadio as a thief and perhaps murderer, it is unlikely that he would know about the trunk, as Drake or Tinker & Skyles might."

I couldn't see any holes in that logic, so I switched gears. "All right, then, maybe this has nothing to do with collector mania. Maybe there's something in Pogue's letter to Mac that presents a danger to the killer, and the killer knew the letter was in the trunk."

"That possibility had not eluded me," Mac assured us. "However, that would leave us with the question of who, other than a fellow conjuror or collector, knew about the existence of the trunk."

I turned to Lexi. "Did your father know about the trunk? Or your aunt?" *Don't ask me why I asked.*

"Why do you ask?"

"Just covering the bases."

"I suppose they both did. Granddad owned it for decades. He once told me he bought it at an auction after Blackstone Jr. died in the late 1990s. But Dad and Aunt Sable wouldn't know about the letter inside, unless Granddad told them—and you know he wasn't on speaking terms with Dad. Anyway, I refuse to believe that either of them had anything to do with the theft of the magician's trunk, much less Granddad's murder."

That created a silence, which Mac filled by saying:

"You did well to separate the two in your thoughts, Alexandra. It may be that the murder and the theft are not related. And there is one other possibility we cannot rule out." *I'm going to hate this.* "And that is that the theft of the trunk was a crime of opportunity. Perhaps someone broke into the store with no particular object in mind other than finding something to steal, and the trunk presented itself."

I was getting a headache.

PILLOW TALK LATER that night at Chez Cody:

"I suspect the witch." That was Lynda.

"Why?"

"Just on general principles. Not that I have anything against pagans, but she pointed a gun at my husband. That could have been a clever red herring to hide the fact that she broke into the store and stole the trunk herself."

"That sounds like something Mac should have come up with."

"Thank you, darling. Did I tell you I bought the kiddoes' Halloween costumes today?"

Chapter Seven
Odd Man In

"A GUN?" POPCORN was enthralled, her green eyes wide. "The woman's a witch. Why didn't she just hex you?"

"That's a stereotype," I told her. "Anyway, once Quant realized it was Pogue's granddaughter and friends making a late-night visit, she put the firearm away. And then she told us—"

It was the morning after. I could have stretched out the story, built up the suspense as I told the tale of our some-times-harrowing evening at the magic shop, but I was hoping we could get some actual SBU work done so I kept it straight to the point. But I didn't leave out the gun.

At the end, Popcorn downed java and said: "I love my Oscar, but this is a McCabe case if I ever saw one: murder and magic."

"McCabe & Cody," I said, going into autocorrect.

My cell rang before Popcorn could amend herself.

"I bet that's Mac," she said.

"Good morning, old boy," he boomed. "I'm patching you into a three-way call with Oscar."

My irreplaceable (though occasionally insubordinate) assistant waved goodbye, then shut the door behind her as her main squeeze came on the line.

"Hi, Jeff. I was just telling Mac that Adrian Pogue was all over me yesterday. Like I should solve his father's murder yesterday. And by the way, he says, why haven't the autopsy results been announced?" The *Observer* that morning contained no hint of Arly Eppensteiner's preliminary conclusion about the homicide of Septimus Pogue, true to Tall Rawls's promise. "I threw that one back in Arly's court, where it belongs. Maybe he'll get her to move up the paperwork to make it official. Anyway, what have you got, Mac?"

"I might ask you the same," Mac parried.

"Show me yours first."

This could get ugly.

Giving in, Mac provided Oscar with a complete account of our encounters with the Pogues and the adventure on Mulberry Street, ending with: "Although I think their involvement unlikely, it is worth the minor effort required to establish whether Logan Drake or Tinker & Skyles were in Erin on the day Septimus died. That is the sort of thing your personnel excel at."

In numbers Erin's police force is commensurate with the small size of the town, but they're all good officers. And the assistant chief, Lt. Col. L. Jack Gibbons, is tops.

"I'll add that chore to the list," Oscar said. "We're already looking into that John Rentz guy that Sable Pogue accused of abusing the deceased. Adrian sicced us on him."

"Excellent," Mac said. "Now it is your turn. Who signed in at Elysian Gardens as visitors to Septimus the day he died?"

"Sable Pogue, who you know; Dr. Thomas Abington, who was the dead man's primary care physician; and Cindy LeVan, who was his former daughter-in-law, Adrian Pogue's ex-wife. Ring any chimes for you?"

Before Mac could answer, I said: "Dr. Abington would have easy access to fentanyl and know how to get it into the line."

"We encountered Dr. Abington in that 'woman in red' business," Mac reminded Oscar, whom I'm pretty sure didn't need reminding. "He is one of Dr. Eppensteiner's part-time assistant coroners."

If skepticism could be heard over the phone, I'm pretty sure Oscar would have hurt both my ear drums.

"What would be his motive?" he asked me after a pause.

"Do I have to do all your work for you?"

"Either love or money is the most likely motivation, no matter who the killer is," Mac said, as if we hadn't been down this road a couple of dozen times before. I had a flitting thought that somebody might think the opposite of love was a pretty good reason to kill somebody, but it got away from me as Mac went on: "I was just about to call Ms. Farleigh and ask about the contents of Septimus's will."

"Have at it," Oscar said.

After disconnecting from the Chief, Mac asked me to stay on the line while he called Phoebe Farleigh, of Farleigh & Farleigh, whose father before her had represented Septimus Pogue for years. The aggressive young barrister had taken the venerable Main Street firm (her father was originally the second Farleigh, in partnership with *his* father) into criminal defense work. Now the rumor was that she wanted to jump to the other side of the fence by running against Sussex County prosecutor Marvin Slade in the 2024 election. But I figured the odds on that happening weren't high; she seemed to like defense work and I presume it paid the bills.

A harassed PA quickly put Mac through to her.

"Professor McCabe! Always a pleasure. How can I help you? I hope you haven't been arrested."

"I have not yet had that pleasure, Ms. Farleigh. I was hoping that you would confirm for me the contents of Septimus's will. It will become public knowledge eventually anyway. Alexandra Pogue, whom you know is the executor, has already told me what she believes it says."

"And you think her grandfather might have misled her? That's why you're asking?"

"Let us say, rather, that Alexandra might have misunderstood, or there might be provisions of which she is unaware."

"Well, that's not unheard of, I must admit. I've seen executors who were shocked at what they were left—or what they weren't left. But I'm meeting with Lexi this afternoon regarding the will, and she won't be surprised. And since I know you to be a person of integrity, and a good friend of my late client, I don't mind confirming for you now what she can tell you in a few hours: You get his prized magician's trunk and its contents, Lexi gets certain named items—"

That would be the cat, the magic collection, and the Checker cab.

"—and the rest, which I gather is a rather substantial amount, gets split between his two children."

"There were no other heirs, then."

"No."

"Did he indicate to you any plans to change his will?"

"He did not. We did review it a few years ago when I joined the firm and my father moved into semi-retirement, but Mr. Pogue made no changes at that time, nor did he indicate to me recently a wish to do so."

"OF COURSE, THAT in no way establishes that Septimus did not tell someone else he planned to change his final testament," Mac told me after he thanked Farleigh and signed off.

"Like Adrian, for example," I said.

"For example."

"And Adrian is pushing Oscar hard to find the killer, which almost proves his guilt!" At least, in one of Mac's books it would.

"On the other hand," Mac volleyed back, "perhaps the only guilt he feels is the guilt of the prodigal son."

"Then there's Adrian's ex-wife, Cindy LeVan," I mused, moving on. "She visited Septimus the day he died. How odd is that, given the 'ex' in front of 'wife'?"

"Not all that odd. Family dynamics are complicated. At any rate, Ms. LeVan presumably had no financial motive, and surely any animus she might have toward her former father-in-law would be satisfied by visiting him to observe the pitiable state to which he had sunk."

The Cody brain kicked into high gear then. "Don't be so sure she had no money motive. Suppose she gets alimony from Adrian. That's not always the case, but it does happen. If Adrian is in financial straits, wouldn't he have trouble paying her—a problem that would disappear if he inherited a pile? And maybe Septimus told her during the visit that he was going to cut his son out of the will, thinking that would please her."

"And she had fentanyl with her?"

"Maybe she's a recreational user."

Disbelief was writ large on the McCabe visage. "Perhaps you gave up your fiction-writing ambitions too soon, old boy. Would you be available to visit Adrian Pogue with me this afternoon?"

I'd been trying, with mixed success, to spend less time away from the office now that I had a staff to whom I should give a good example. "I suppose I can call it lunch hour," I said.

"BY THUNDER, THE MAN lives in a flying saucer!"

Mac's exclamation was understandable. Like his daughter, the animal communicator lived in a woodsy area. Unlike her A-frame, his dwelling was silver and, yes, looked like a UFO on metal legs anchored in concrete. It had oval-shaped windows running all around it, some covered by curtains on the inside.

"It's called a Futuro House and it was pre-fabbed," I informed Mac. We were in my wheelhouse now. "A Finnish architect came up with this design in the late 1960s.[7] I think fewer than a hundred were made. The original idea was that they were to be chalets, vacation homes in the mountains."

I was on a roll, happy for the chance to tell my polymath brother-in-law something he didn't know. Buildings have always fascinated me, maybe because my father sold houses for a living. "I occasionally read about Futuros that

---

[7]To be specific, Matti Suuronen created the Futuro in 1968. Sometimes a color other than silver, such as yellow or orange, a Futuro House or Futuro Pod is made of fiberglass-reinforced plastic. It's 13 feet high, 26 feet in diameter, and is said to accommodate eight people. Now you know.

have been repurposed, or still used as private homes, or rented out through Airbnb. Somehow it flew under my radar that there's one in Erin. But now that I know there is, I can't say I'm surprised that our local Dr. Doolittle lives in it."

Just as we got out of Mac's monstrous motorcar and approached the house, a trap door in the front lowered to reveal steps. Adrian Pogue descended and walked toward us, wearing not a space suit but old jeans and a plaid shirt.

"What do you think of my house?"

"I find it, er, extraordinary," Mac said, with some restraint.

"And the best part is, I power the whole thing—the entire house—on a battery I bought out of a junked Tesla in Georgia. Now I'm entirely off the grid, no utility bills."

Maybe this guy isn't as crazy as he looks, sounds, and acts. Based on our average monthly gas and electric bill of $250 at the Cody manor, that Tesla battery would pay for itself in—

". . . weighs over a thousand pounds," Pogue was saying, describing the battery when I tuned back in. "Come on in."

We mounted the five steps into the house, with him behind us. Inside was one big room with built-in furniture around the walls, including couches that must have folded out into beds. Seated on one of them was the plump dyed brunette I'd seen holding Adrian's hand at the Lyceum.

"This is my wife, Cindy LeVan," he said.

She stood up and put out her hand. "Ex-wife. He keeps forgetting."

Pogue ignored the niggling detail.

"I hope you're here to tell me that you know who killed my father," he said while Mac and I shook the LeVan hand.

He didn't tell us to sit down.

"Not quite," Mac said. "Did you know that you are one of the major heirs, along with your daughter and sister?"

"I am?"

Pogue was either shocked or a good actor. I could flip a coin as to which.

"You are," I assured him.

"That's nice of the old man, but I wish he'd given me the money when he was still alive, and I could have thanked him for it." Pogue seemed more peeved than elated. "I would have made him a partner and we'd both be rich by now. National franchises are a goldmine." He probably didn't know that the Hertz car-rental franchise went into bankruptcy in 2020, although they're doing better now.

Then he revved up.

"You're wasting your time talking about motives, like some TV whodunit." *Or like McCabe & Cody.* "What about his old partner, Clay Belmont? I hear the other partner, Ira Brown, died not long ago. Maybe Belmont wasted both of them over some long-ago dispute."

Mac raised an eyebrow.

"That's ridiculous," Cindy LeVan snapped. "Dad always called those two his blood brothers. Besides, even assuming that Clay Belmont is a homicidal maniac, why wait decades to settle some business-related score?"

"Revenge is a dish best served cold. And now that I think of it, I'm pretty sure Brown was killed by a hit-and-run driver who was never caught."

I made a mental note of that: Ira Brown didn't die of old age.

Mac interrupted this love fest with:

"Neither of the Belmonts signed the guest register at Elysian Gardens the day Septimus died, but some other familiar names appear in that book. Dr. Thomas Abington, for one. We saw him at the memorial."

"Name sounds familiar," Pogue said. "He might have been Pop's doc."

"He was," LeVan snipped.

"You also signed in that day, Ms. LeVan," Mac noted.

She nodded. "I visited him a lot. We always got along. Seeing him on his last day was a mixed blessing, I suppose. He looked terrible. It was no surprise to me that he died, just that it wasn't on God's time." She shook her head. "I still can't believe it."

"You saw nothing out of the ordinary that day, then?"

"I wasn't exactly looking for it, was I?"

Mac bowed slightly. "I take your point, Ms. LeVan." He turned to her ex. "Do you remember a magician's trunk that your father owned?"

"The one that he told me a million times belonged to what's his name?"

"Blackstone," I informed him.

"Yeah, him. Sure, I remember."

"It was stolen from the former Magic Unlimited shop on the day your father died," Mac said.

"No shit!" Then Pogue showed a surprisingly practical side by saying, "It could be worth a lot of money because of its provenance, but you couldn't exactly market that on eBay or EBTH."

Mac raised a quizzical eyebrow.

"Everything But The House," I translated the initials. "It's an online auction house. Very popular for estate sales."

"Collectors are everywhere, no matter what the hobby is," Cindy LeVan said. "I'm sure a thief who knew what they were doing could find a buyer by putting out the word in the right places."

But that's not what happened. The trunk magically reappeared at the Lyceum Theater that evening. And Mac and Kate's son, my nephew Brian, is the one who found it.

Chapter Eight
The Magician's Trunk

ENCOURAGED BY MAC'S mom, who's a retired soap opera actor, my now-19-year-old nephew played Tiny Tim in the 2018 production of *A Christmas Carol* at SBU's Davenport-Lattimore Bijou Theatre[8] and performed as a ventriloquist in the Lyceum Players' "A Night at the Music Hall."[9] Now Brian is a theater major at SBU. And for the upcoming production of *The Man Who Came to Dinner*, with Mac typecast as the outlandish Sheridan Whiteside, he was not only acting in the play but part of the crew building the sets before rehearsals were to begin in a few weeks. That's how he happened to be backstage and spotted the trunk that looked to him like the one his father was bloviating about at dinner.

"Well done, my boy!" Mac told him. "You are your father's son."

"I'd better be."

Mac had picked me up on the way to the Lyceum, making me leave hearth and home as soon as he received Brian's text with an image of the trunk. The size wasn't obvious from the picture when Mac showed it to me, but I later

---

[8] See *Too Many Clues* (MX Publishing, 2019).
[9] See *Murderers' Row* (MX Publishing, 2020).

learned that the trunk measured 32 inches long, 17 inches deep and 23 inches high at the highest part of its curved top. Whatever color it had started out with, it was dark now with the patina of age.

"Are you sure it's the trunk you're looking for?" harumphed Lafcadio Figg in his usual pompous manner. Between him and Mac, I'm not sure which one is oil, and which one is water. And yet, they are both Sherlockians, and this wasn't the first time Figg cast his *bête noire* (Mac's term) in a play. He allowed Mac to portray Mycroft Holmes in the Lyceum's inaugural production, *1895*, which Mac wrote based on a Sherlock Holmes story called "The Adventure of the Bruce-Partington Plans." (Henry Knox Wilcox, writing in the *Observer*, called Mac "convincingly obnoxious" in the role.)

"Quite confident, Lafcadio," Mac said. "This is indeed the Blackstone Senior trunk that was stolen from what was once Magic Unlimited. Although I have not seen it in many years, I could never forget it. The real question is, what is it doing here?"

"Here" was behind the curtain, where all the magic of the theater that the audience sees gives way on the other side of the stage to canvas, wood, saws, and hammers. ("Pay no attention to the crew behind the curtain," someone should say.) I hadn't been backstage at the Lyceum since that *1895* business. The place was littered with actors at the moment, including my ace staffer Riley St. James, who was to play June Stanley opposite Brian as her brother Richard. The young Stanleys are members of the Ohio family upon whom Sheridan Whiteside descends at Christmas.

"How should I know what it's doing here?" Figg protested, even though he hadn't been asked. "Surely you don't think that I had anything to do with purloining the trunk and bringing it here, Sebastian?"

That's not what Mac said. But anybody using the word "purloining" should be guilty of something.

"Nobody has better access to the theater than you," I said.

"This is not exactly a secure location," Mac mused. "There was no one to stop us—or anyone else—from entering this evening. The door was unlocked, and the stage crew occupied. I imagine it would not have been difficult for someone to wander in here in an elementary disguise and leave the trunk so as to implicate Lafcadio."

"I'm not implicated!" Figg roared. "And I don't need you to defend me. Stay out of this, Sebastian."

"You did show a strong interest in Pogue's baseball card collection," I pointed out.

"What of it?" The stocky Figg pulled himself up to his full five-foot-five. "We don't even know that there are any baseball cards in that trunk, assuming that it does belong to the late Mr. Pogue."

"We can open it and find out," Brian suggested, earning a murderous look from Figg. "The latch is open, so it's not locked."

"That would be inappropriate and perhaps illegal without permission of the owner," Figg said.

"I am the owner," Mac said.

"Not yet, you aren't. The will has not yet gone through the necessary legalities."

"Right you are!" Mac said to my surprise. He pulled out his cell and clicked on one of the "Recents."

"Mac?" came the voice of Lexi Pogue. Mac put her on speakerphone.

"Hello, Alexandra. I have the pleasure of informing you that we have found the magician's trunk."

"What? Where?"

Before she could ask when, how, and who, Mac briefly explained the situation, ending with: "May we have your permission, as executor, to open the trunk?"

"Yes! Of course. You know that Granddad willed you its contents anyway." So did all the readers of the *Observer* know that. "But I'd like to see it when you do. Put me on Facebook Video so I can watch."

He did so, then handed his cell to Brian to hold while he opened the trunk.

Inside was the strangest assortment of things I'd ever seen, including a top hat, a crystal ball, some 1950s era baseball cards, a set of handcuffs, and an imitation thumb.

"This moment has deep emotional resonance for me," Mac told Lexi (and the rest of us by extension). "Almost all of these items that Septimus wanted me to have relate to magic effects that he taught me. The handcuffs from which he taught me to escape belonged to Houdini, incidentally, and the top hat from which I once pulled a stuffed rabbit was Thurston's.[10] Perhaps these envelopes hold something of similar significance."

While Mac reached for said envelopes, I took photos of everything inside the trunk with my phone.

---

[10] Howard Thurston is sometimes called the last great stage illusionist. An Ohio native with an international fame, he performed annually in Cincinnati from 1907 to 1932. So far as is known, he was not related to the Thurston with whom Dr. Watson played billiards.—*S. McC.*

"Why are you doing that, Uncle Jeff?" Brian wanted to know.

"I have no idea," I said. But it was a good thing that I did it.

"These are insurance policies," Mac announced, holding up the contents of the envelopes. "Two million-dollar policies from the Lexington Mutual Insurance Company, one naming Ira Brown as the beneficiary and one naming Clayton Belmont."

"Too late for Ira Brown," I said.

What was not in the trunk was the fireproof box that Septimus Pogue told Sebastian McCabe to either open or destroy, depending on whether or not he had been murdered.

Chapter Nine
Insurance

MAGICIAN MURDERED; MISSING TRUNK FOUND was the double-barreled headline at the top of the *Erin Observer & News-Ledger* on Friday morning. This was no surprise to your favorite sleuths, for Johanna Rawls had called Mac the evening before. Hard up against a deadline, she wanted a comment about the official finding of homicide that Dr. Eppensteiner emailed to Oscar on her way out the door for the day. Oscar had called Johanna, who called Eppensteiner and then Mac for comment. Mac, in turn, informed the reporter that he'd found the trunk.

"Why did you tell her that?" I asked when he called to loop me in. "The trunk didn't even come up when she crashed our pow-wow in Oscar's office."

"As Holmes said, 'The press, Watson, is a most valuable institution, if only you know how to use it.' I made no mention to Ms. Rawls of the missing fireproof box, which will keep the player on the side—whether that be the killer or someone else—in doubt as to whether we know about it."

Johanna's front-page story the next day began:

> The death of 92-year-old Septimus Pogue
> was ruled a homicide by Sussex County Coroner

Dr. Arlene Eppensteiner on Thursday, the same day a missing trunk belonging to the dead man was found backstage at the Lyceum Theater.

Eppensteiner undertook the autopsy at the request of the Pogue family via St. Benignus University professor and mystery writer Sebastian McCabe, a close friend of the deceased. Family members and McCabe declined to say why the autopsy was requested.

"The cause of death was an overdose of fentanyl," Eppensteiner said. "Given that Mr. Pogue wasn't prescribed the drug, and there was no indication he was a recreational drug user, his death was no accident."

Pogue died on October 18 at the Elysian Gardens nursing home, where he had been a resident since early last year. Elysian officials declined to comment.

"We have opened a homicide investigation and will pursue it with all the resources at our command," said Erin Police Chief Oscar Hummel.

In a curious twist, a missing magician's trunk once belonging to famed conjuror Harry Blackstone Sr. and most recently to Septimus Pogue mysteriously turned up last evening at the Lyceum Theater.

"No one has any idea how it got there," said McCabe, who has helped Erin police solve several murders. "When last seen it was at the location of the now-closed Magic Unlimited shop, which Mr. Pogue operated for many years until illness forced him to enter the nursing home."

And so on. The rest of the story recycled some background on Pogue from Frank Woodford's column (which itself was recycled from earlier stories) and described a bit of the memorial service. There was a tagline at the end that said, "*Bernard J. Silverstein contributed to this report.*"

"I like the part about how Mac has 'helped Erin police solve several murders' instead of 'handed the killers to Oscar on a platinum platter,'" I told Lynda at breakfast. She was deep into her crossword puzzle, having already read the story while I poured cereal for five.

"That's just to keep him humble," she said.

We both laughed.

Then Lynda read a clue out loud, which was my cue to chip in.

"'Queen of mysteries.' Hmm."

"Agatha Christie," I said, feeling that to be a no-brainer.

"No, it's six letters, and the first one is 'E' and the last one is 'Y.' ELLERY! It's Ellery Queen, the writer and detective, one of Mac's favorites. Thank you, darling."

"Glad to help."

POPCORN HANDED ME my morning decaf and took her accustomed seat in front of my desk. We've been doing this dance for so many years the chair must have an impression in the shape of her rump. Although I've never checked.

"What are the kids up to today?" I asked.

"Riley is getting pictures of our 'Banned Books Week' activities to post on all known social media along with a story.

Sylvester is working on a story for *Ben* about our Lady Dragons going into the basketball season with a winning look."

"My favorite team."

"Those are the highlights until something more urgent runs downhill, Boss. So, when are you and Mac going to see Oscar?"

"What makes you think we're going to see Oscar?"

She held up the *Observer* with its headline blaring **MURDERED** as the second word.

"Oh. Well, that's up to Mac. He may have something else up his sleeve." *Nothing Up My Sleeve* was one of Mac's Damon Devlin novels—the murder of a magician onstage during his act with thousands in the audience watching and no one near him—but I pushed that thought aside. "I mean, he may want to go see somebody else in the case. I can take an early lunch break."

"Don't sound so defensive about getting out of the office, Boss." Popcorn imbibed caffeine from her mug. "You and Mac helping my honey solve cases is good publicity for SBU." *My honey?* "Besides, you never turn off your cell, so you're really working 'round the clock."

"I like the way you think, Pokorny."

"OSCAR CALLED TO say that Tinker & Skyles performed as usual in Las Vegas the day that Septimus died, which leaves them out," Mac informed me when I dropped by Herbert Hall in late morning.

"You've never heard of a hit man?"

"Logan Drake," he steamed on, "also performed that evening—but at the Forty Thieves, only an hour's drive away from Erin. He told Col. Gibbons that previous to his performance he was consumed with various chores, alone, including practicing a new illusion. That assertion is not particularly important. We know that Septimus was pronounced dead by a staff physician at 7:05 P.M., having been found a few minutes earlier, and that he had not been dead for more than an hour. Logan Drake's performance began at 7:30. Mr. Drake must have arrived some time earlier, given that one does not simply walk onto a stage with no preparation. As a practical matter, I find it implausible that he could have committed the murder."

"Implausibility never stopped us before. Did Drake have any reason you know of to steal the trunk and then plant it where it would incriminate Figg?"

"Alas, no! Of course, the theft of the magician's trunk could have been a crime of opportunity brought about by Septimus's death but carried out by someone other than the killer."

"Of course," I agreed. This notion had been trotted out already. Shifting gears, I said, "I find it suspicious that Figg so adamantly rejected your support last night."

"Really, Jefferson?" He chuckled. "I find it quite in character. Lafcadio was simply being Lafcadio. He is an egomaniac, not a nincompoop. If he stole the trunk because of an inexplicable affection for baseball cards, he would scarcely have left it at the Lyceum where it could be—and indeed was—easily found and connected to him. No, the thief-cum-murderer put the trunk there in an attempt to direct us away from something or someone else."

"Like whom or what?"

"That is the question, old boy! Perhaps directing us away from the Pogue family."

"What makes you say that?"

"Just that it does, in fact, direct us away from the Pogue family. I said 'perhaps.'" He gave that a think, smoking a mental cigar, then changed direction. "There is no way to know what was in that trunk when it was residing at the magic shop. It could have held something quite valuable—either a unique collectible or something more tangible, such as cash—but that is sheer speculation at this point. What we do know is what *was* there when it turned up at the Lyceum."

He held up the two envelopes containing insurance policies. "You will recall Septimus's direction in his letter: 'Some of those contents you can keep, some you will know to redirect appropriately.' Clearly, these fall into the latter category. If these policies are not expired, they give the beneficiaries a motive for murder."

"Except for the slight fact that one of the beneficiaries is himself expired," I said.

"Well, there is that. Oscar confirmed for me that Ira Brown was run over by an unknown driver who has not been apprehended. The death vehicle was a silver Honda Civic, a very common model, and none of the three witnesses was able to see the full license plate number. However, Oscar said one of the three—apparently the one with the best angle of vision—reported that Mr. Brown almost threw himself in the path of the automobile as it approached while exceeding the speed limit."

"I remember that business now! The victim's name meant nothing to me at the time. It happened on Front Street at four o'clock in the afternoon. Brown had been drinking at Gatsby's. So that has nothing to do with the case at hand."

"Most likely not—or if so, only indirectly."

"Did Oscar say anything about John Rentz, the world's worst nursing home attendant?"

"He said the young man was off due to illness the day that Septimus was poisoned. Mr. Rentz claimed to have COVID-like symptoms, but in the end did not have the disease."

"Oh, come on! How suspicious is that?"

"Not very. For one thing, Mr. Rentz is often absent, receives poor performance reviews, and the Elysian Gardens personnel director assured Oscar in confidence that he will soon be looking for other employment. For another, the sort of murderer you posit—one who acts out of the same warped impulse that caused him to be verbally abusive—would scarcely be likely to think far enough ahead to create an alibi for himself. And surely, he would run the risk that someone would see him enter the victim's room on a day that he was supposed to be ill."

"I never said he was a criminal mastermind."

Also, there was something about the name John that bothered me. Was there another John in this case? Before I could make a mental note to think about thinking about that, Mac caught my attention with:

"In any case, Jefferson, I think a visit to the Collier Agency is in order. That was the insurance brokerage firm that sold Septimus the policies, according to a sticker affixed to them."

"Wait a minute. Isn't that Wes Collier's outfit now? The guy who used to date Kate back in college before you showed up?"

"Did he?"

"You know he did!"

WES COLLIER WAS a broad-faced glad-hander in his early 50s, with glasses that turn dark in the light even when it's not that bright. I always find that annoying. A couple of years older than Kate, who is my big sister by 18 months, he seemed like a guy who would buy you a drink in a bar even if he didn't know you—but then he'd start asking if you had enough insurance. Collier remembered me as Kate's brother, which helped to open the door a little when we showed up at his office. Mac opened it a bit wider by mentioning Oscar, implying that we were acting officially.

"Yeah, the policies are still good," Collier said. "All of them."

"You mean both of them." Mac hates imprecision of grammar.

"I mean all the policies where Brown, Belmont, and Pogue insured each other." Mac arched an eyebrow, to which Collier explained: "Partner insurance is very common in business. But I remember my father talking about how odd it was that they kept it up after they sold their funeral home. Dad was a lodge brother of Ira Brown—that's how he got the business."

"The late Mr. Brown," I specified.

"Right."

"So, Clayton Belmont and Septimus each received one million dollars under Mr. Brown's policies when he died?" Mac said.

"Right again." Collier sat back, hands folded over his ample tummy. "Maybe I shouldn't be telling you this."

"No, it's fine," I assured him.

"Since Mr. Brown is deceased, does the money that otherwise would have gone to him upon Septimus's death go to his heirs instead?" Mac asked.

Collier shook his head. "No, no. Pogue named what's called a 'contingent beneficiary' in case Brown died before him. Are you ready for this? Said contingent was Clayton Belmont. So, Belmont will get the money from Pogue's insurance that would have gone to Ira Brown as well as the payout under the policy naming him as primary beneficiary."

"And what about Mr. Brown's policy naming Septimus as the beneficiary?"

"Ah. That's different. Since Pogue outlived Brown, even though he died later, Lexington Mutual will write a check to Pogue and it will become part of his estate."

I could tell he was enjoying sharing the ins and outs and ups and downs of the insurance game.

"By the way," Collier added, "how's Kate?"

"Fine," I said.

"Excellent!" Mac assured him with gusto.

Chapter Ten

Last Man Standing

MAC COULDN'T FIRE up his cigar fast enough when we got out of Collier's office, a brick house on a section of String Street where zoning made it possible for a lot of houses to be repurposed to small businesses.

"What did you get out of all that, Jefferson?"

"A headache."

"Hmph." He opened the door of his Chevy, which took up almost two normal-sized parking spaces on the street. "Please specify."

Speaking as I was climbing into the car, I said: "On the one hand, Septimus Pogue's son and daughter profit more financially than we knew from his death, since Septimus got a wad of money under Ira Brown's insurance policy. Yet, we still have the problem of why kill a man that everybody agreed was circling the drain"—that was a bit insensitive, I admit—"to get an inheritance that so far as we know wouldn't change in a few weeks or months."

"'So far as we know' being the key phrase," Mac interjected.

"Granted. On the other hand, Clay Belmont is raking it in from the deaths of his two former partners. He was named in one of Ira Brown's life insurance policies as the beneficiary and in one of Septimus Pogue's as the contingent beneficiary, which he will now—I'd better take this."

I had a call on my cell. It was "Morris Kindle of the Associated Press here." That's how the veteran newshound introduces himself every time, as if I didn't know he was the southwest Ohio AP guy after—what?—at least 15 years of calling me to ask St. Benignus-related questions.

"I have a press release here from a group called Stop the Lies in the Skies. They're calling on SBU to disinvite an upcoming speaker, Dr. Maria Lamplighter from NASA, who they say is part of a cover-up hiding the truth about Unidentified Aerial Phenomena, formerly known as UFOs, and aliens on earth. They say if you don't cancel her, they will shout her down."

I didn't even have to think about that one. Grace Langley, the chair of our board of trustees; Grant Kingsley, our president; and Lesley Saylor-Mackie, executive vice president and provost, were on the same page, coming from the same place, or however you want to say there was no daylight between them on this issue.

"SBU is in the business of opening minds, Morrie, not closing them," I said. *Hey, that's not bad!* "Dr. Lamplighter is a distinguished scientist who also holds an advanced degree in theology. She was invited by Campus Ministry to share her thoughts about 'God and the Galaxies.'" I was pretty sure that Lynda's best gal pal, science fiction buff and campus minister Sister Mary Margaret Malone (aka Triple M) arranged that. "Anybody who tries to shout her down will be politely but forcefully escorted out." No need to mention that

Chief Ed Decker and uber-competent Assistant Chief Aurelia Banfield of the St. Benignus University Police were already getting geared up for the November event.

After a few follow-up questions, we bid each other a fond farewell.

"Bravo," Mac told me.

"Thanks, but I didn't exactly work up a sweat on that one." By this time, we were on the road. "Let's recap: Septimus Pogue was murdered, and his magician's trunk was stolen. We may be looking for a murderer-thief or a murderer and a thief. Septimus asked you to have an autopsy conducted and destroy something that was in the trunk if he was not murdered—but said object is missing. What was not missing from the trunk was two insurance policies leaving a million bucks each to his old partners, the late Ira Brown and the very much alive Clay Belmont. That about it?"

"That is an excellent summary."

"Okay, just checking. Where to now?"

"To pay a call on Clayton Belmont. I programmed his address into my phone this morning. Even then I thought a chat might be useful. Now, of course, it is imperative. I trust that he will be at home, although I shall not call ahead, preferring to have the advantage of surprise."

"You think maybe he snuck into Elysian Gardens and injected his old partner's line with fentanyl?"

"I think, Jefferson, that we would be foolish indeed not to talk to him."

CLAY BELMONT LIVED in a two-story brick Colonial home in one of Erin's fancier neighborhoods, not far from where the ill-starred Bainbridge clan lived—when they were all alive.

He came to the door in response to Mac's ring, wearing khaki cargo pants but looking natty in a checked flannel shirt and slip-on shoes. Up close, it wasn't hard to believe he was 86—but a hale and hearty 86. He didn't seem like a man on, say for example, a painkiller like fentanyl.

"Let's sit in the living room. Want a drink? It's five o'clock somewhere."

Like Rome, maybe.

When we declined, he shrugged his shoulders, and led us into a comfortable room with stuffed leather chairs and sofas. I would say it was neat as a pin, but I've never known why pins are considered neat.

"I have a good housekeeper," he said, reading my mind. "My wife died almost twenty years ago, God rest her soul."

"I have often wondered whether being constantly surrounded by death inures one to it," Mac said.

"In the funeral home business, you mean? No, it doesn't. Not in my experience as a mortician. But there was satisfaction in being there for people in their time of need." That sounded like a rote line from decades earlier that rolled out of his mouth without stopping by his brain, as ready-made as a Futuro House. Belmont stretched out his feet on an ottoman next to a small table that held an ashtray. There was already a rocks glass at his side, almost filled with a dark liquid and no ice, next to a 1.75-liter bottle of Jack Daniel's. He gave the glass a lift. Dutch courage? "So, McCabe, are you here to talk about what happened with the old firm, Pogue & Belmont?"

"Only to the degree that it might having any bearing on the murder of Septimus Pogue."

Belmont seemed surprised.

"Oh. Well, there's not much to say about the old firm anyway. We made a decent amount of money until those bastards at Hawes & Holder nearly drove us out of business by undercutting our prices. And then our embezzling office manager finished us off. After he did a bunk, we decided to sell out while we could instead of spending all our money just to stay afloat. It was a good business decision."

All that, too, sounded rote. How many times had Belmont told that neatly packaged story over the years?

"You three went your separate ways but remained 'blood brothers.'"

Belmont looked at Mac as if he'd been hit. "What?"

"Adrian Pogue's former wife asserted that Septimus always referred to you and Ira Brown as his blood brothers."

"He did? Well, that's true enough." Belmont gave a hoarse chuckle and pulled a pack of cigarettes out of his pocket. I couldn't remember the last time I'd seen somebody do that indoors. "But, yeah, separate ways. Sep started that magic shop. Maybe he got tired of making money. Ira, who operated a crematorium before he joined us at Pogue & Belmont, became a car salesman of all damned things. I went into the vintage furniture business—buy low, sell high—and I did okay."

Belmont lit a cigarette and took a lusty drag.

That will shorten your life, Clay. And I'm not crazy about the second-hand smoke.

I concentrated on not coughing.

"You said on the phone you're poking into Sep's murder," Belmont told Mac.

"Essentially correct," Mac conceded, "although I would choose other words. I hope that my call has inspired you to give some thought to the obvious question of who killed Septimus Pogue."

The old man blew smoke.

"I heard around town that his son didn't have anything good to say about him. You might look there. On the other hand, sounds like a pretty tricky murder from what I read in the *Observer*. Maybe it was one of his magic pals who wasn't such a pal." He shrugged. "Like you said, separate ways. I haven't talked to Ira and Sep very much in the last thirty years, not at any length."

"And both of them are now dead," I said, in case he hadn't noticed.

"Yeah, well, I heard around town a few weeks back that Sep's number was about up anyway. I kind of wish I'd gone to visit one last time. But I hate nursing homes, even nice ones with fancy names."

"It has come to our intention that you were the beneficiary of insurance policies by both of your late partners, and additionally the contingent beneficiary of Septimus's policy," Mac said. "'Last Man Standing,' as you yourself put it at the memorial service."

It wouldn't be correct to say that Belmont shot daggers at him with his eyes—it was more like swords. "I was feeling pretty down that day, not quite myself. What the hell are you implying, McCabe?"

"I imply nothing. I stated a fact."

"A meaningless fact. I'm the survivor. Somebody had to be."

"A very wealthy survivor," I said.

Belmont gave me his full attention. "Your name is Cody?"

"Yes, sir."

"Well, Cody, you're more annoying than Nero Wolfe here."

What a low blow.

"It is rather unusual to continue partner insurance after a partnership no longer exists, is it not?" Mac asked.

Again, a shrug. "I don't know what's usual or unusual along that line. I just know that we felt we owed it to each other because of what we'd been through together. That's still true, the connection, even though we haven't been in close touch." Clay Belmont was totally honest about that, I realized just now as I typed those words. In fact, everything he told us that day was true—just not complete.

"Fat lot of good the money will do me now," Belmont added. "What next? Are you going to ask me for my alibi?"

"And if we did?" Mac parried.

"Then I'd say tell me when Septimus was killed—I know it was last Wednesday, but what time?"

"His death was discovered in the afternoon, and he had died not long before."

"I was playing poker and drinking bourbon with Lenny Connors, Harvey Anderson, and Roscoe Driscoll at the country club." He didn't need to specify which country club because there's only one in Erin.

"Any luck?" I wondered.

He took a drag on the cigarette before he said, "I lost ten bucks."

Better than losing your life.

"THAT 'FAT LOT of good' line was his way of pointing out that he's no spring chicken and wouldn't have long to enjoy his ill-gotten gains if he were the killer, despite his apparent good health," I noted as I strapped myself into Mac's super-sized vehicle.

"My grandmother is 102 and still driving."

"If I were a betting man, I'd bet she doesn't smoke."

"You would win that wager, old boy."

At which point he lit a cigar. "I will ask Oscar to have his officers see whether Mr. Belmont was signed in at Elysian Gardens on that fateful day, purportedly visiting someone else—despite his avowed detestation of such places—and also show his photo around the staff to see if he looked familiar to anyone. They can also investigate his alibi by talking to his three poker-mates or the bartender. Meanwhile, I believe that we should inquire further into the death of Ira Brown."

"How?"

"We shall talk to his daughter-in-law, Sarah Fink-Brown, his late son's widow. According to the obituary published in the *Observer* upon his death, she is his only survivor."

"What do you mean, 'we'? Count me out. I have to pretend to work for a few hours."

Mac stared for several moments, stunned at this rebellion.

"Come, come, Jefferson, you know that I am lost without my—"

"Don't say it! Just don't say it! All right, I'll go with you. But I have to put in a little face time at the office first. See if Mrs. Fink-Brown can see us at the shank end of the day."

THE HIGHLIGHT OF my workday was a call from J. Randolph Smith, a reporter for *Higher Ed Insider*, just as I had begun to cogitate over a possibly brilliant theory tying the murder to the magician's trunk. The Smith name instantly registered in the Cody memory banks as a pesky fellow who probably wasn't calling for a story about the growth of SBU. At least, that wasn't his plan.

"College enrollment is down 9 percent nationally since 2020," he informed me. "Tuition has skyrocketed over the last three decades while the wages of workers between the ages of 22 and 27 have gone up less than twenty percent. Do you see a connection?"

"I really can't speak to that, Randy. That would be speculative. But what I can tell you is that our enrollment has gone up eight percent over the past three years." No need to mention that put us just slightly above pre-COVID levels. "And, not coincidentally, we haven't increased tuition in two years. We've also added a Master of Health Administration degree and a Master of Arts in Leadership to our program offerings." After cutting a few other programs.

"How did you do it?"

Our president is a retired miliary officer who isn't afraid to cut costs where needed, but also knows how to spend productively—in the marketing and communications area, for example.

"We are laser-focused on delivering a Catholic-based holistic education that equips our graduates for life but also for employment, Randy. That answers the enrollment part. As to keeping tuition under control, it's no coincidence that we have a low administrator-to-faculty ratio and it's getting even lower." *Unlike some competitors I could name.* "That has been one of our president's goals since the beginning of his administration."

And so forth.

"That sounded like fun," Popcorn said, standing in the doorway of my office when I'd finished.

"It was. Our job is telling a story, and that's easy when the story is a good one."

I had a vague feeling I'd said that before. And why not? It was true.

"How long do you think it will take Mac to solve this one, Boss?"

What? Where did that come from?

"Why does everybody always think Mac is the one who's going to figure out whodunit?"

She gave me a look filled with pity and said nothing, so I continued:

"As a matter of fact, I have an idea I want to road test." I stood up. "I'm going to pedal into town. I'll be back within a half-hour."

"Are you going to tell me what's going on?"

"That depends on how this goes."

THE TRIP DOWNTOWN via my trusty Schwinn was a quick one, but more exciting than I like when I almost got hit by a young woman in an SBU hoodie who needs lessons in driving an electric scooter. I made a mental note to vote for Roger Belmont and his anti-scooter crusade. But that was before I got to know him better.

Balls & Strikes is Erin's only purveyor of baseball cards and memorabilia, located on Cherry Street near Broadway. I'd never been inside before, although I had a vague memory that the store opened around the time I arrived in Erin in 1992. I didn't know the proprietor, Ray Palmer.

When I entered the place, which looked like it had been last freshened up during the second Clinton Administration, that made exactly two of us there including Palmer. Decorated with posters and packed with boxes of baseball cards old and new, the other inventory on display included inscribed bats, balls, and antique fanwear brandishing team names that no longer exist (e.g., Cleveland Indians).

Palmer was a short, stocky man with a round face and equally round glasses who covered his mostly hairless head with a Cincinnati Reds baseball cap. At his apparent age he could have been collecting Social Security. And I thought maybe that was his income source, given the lack of trade. Standing behind a counter below a poster of legendary Cincinnati Reds slugger and Erin resident Brett McGee—whose spouse owns Bobbie McGee's Sports Bar on Market Street— he flashed a smile as I entered.

"Hi, can I help you?" was his opening line.

"I hope so. I don't know anything about baseball cards."

And very little about baseball, although I've been known to take in an Erin Eagles game.[11]

Palmer smiled. "Good thing I do, then. Hey, wait! You're Jeff Cody, aren't you?"

"Guilty."

"I've read all your books!"

The warm glow that gave me was as unfamiliar as it was welcome. I'm fairly well known around town from my day job, which occasionally involves media appearances, but I don't get huzzahs from readers very often. My entire fan

---

[11] See "Foul Ball" in *Murderers' Row* (MX Publishing, 2020).

base for these chronicles would fit in my New Beetle Final Edition.

"Thanks," I told Palmer.

And thank you, too, dear reader!

"How can I help you, Jeff?"

I pulled out my phone, went to the picture gallery, and called up images of the baseball cards I'd photographed in the Blackstone trunk along with the other trunk contents. The cards were spread out so you could see the smiling faces of the players, almost all of whom I was sure were no longer among the living.

"These are some old baseball cards that a friend of mine just inherited," I explained.

"McCabe, right? Did these cards belong to that dead magician friend of his?"

Clearly, Palmer was a close reader of the *Observer*.

"Right. As you can see, they're from the 1950s. What I want to know is, are they valuable?"

"Is there a Mickey Mantle rookie card in there?"

"If there were, I wouldn't be asking that question." A little over a year earlier, a mint condition 1952 Mantle card had sold at auction for $12.6 million. I may not know baseball cards from applesauce, but I know dollar signs.

Palmer studied the photos on my phone for what seemed like forever and a half. His eyes seemed to widen a bit, which I took as a good sign.

Finally, he gave the phone back to me and said: "Yep, they're valuable. These are Bowman cards. Not as well-known as Topps to the general public, but popular with collectors. Topps bought the brand in 1955 and buried it until 1989. I'd be willing to give your friend two thousand dollars for the lot."

"Only two grand!"

"Okay, twenty-five hundred."

"I'll tell him," I said. "But he won't be selling until after the case is closed and the murderer tried."

"IT WAS A good theory for about half an hour," I told Popcorn back at the office in a confessional mood. I'd returned to find her reading one of her beloved Rosamund DeLacey[12] romance novels, *Love's Burning Ache*, but I was too down to rag her about her taste in lunch-hour literature. "I figured that somebody knew Pogue had some valuable baseball cards and killed to get them. But the cards in question aren't exactly super-valuable as those things go. Who would murder an old man for twenty-five hundred dollars?"

She stared at me. "Are you kidding? People get killed every day for five dollars."

"Not in Erin."

"Well, there is that. People get murdered in Erin for much better motives. But there's an even bigger problem with your theory, Boss: If somebody killed Septimus Pogue for the baseball cards, why would they still be in the trunk, and the trunk at the theater?"

"Er, um, well . . ."

Her eyes widened. "You thought Figg did it, and that's why the trunk was at the Lyceum."

"Maybe 'hoped' is a more accurate word."

---

[12] Whose true identity as a member of the SBU administration is revealed in *Bookmarked for Murder* (MX Publishing, 2015).

Chapter Eleven
Down a Rabbit Hole?

SARAH FINK-BROWN WAS chief of nursing at St. Hildegarde Health, Erin's hospital and a regional leader that punches above its weight in cancer care. A small woman with dark hair cut short, she met us in her office.

"No, I didn't know anything about those insurance policies," she said. "If Howard did, he never mentioned it to me." Dr. Howard Brown was her late husband. "What does this have to do with anything?"

"If only we knew!" Mac said fervently. "I am poking and prodding in hopes of unearthing some clue as to why Septimus Pogue was murdered."

"I don't see how I can help with that." She spoke briskly without being rude.

"Your father-in-law died only a few weeks ago, killed in an auto accident in which a witness indicated he deliberately put himself the path of the oncoming vehicle. I do not dismiss coincidence, but I do raise an eyebrow at it."

Fink-Brown's eyes misted a bit. "That was a cruel irony. Howard was only 41 when he died of COVID. He was immunocompromised. Whereas Ira had the virus in '22 and sailed through it, then he got in front of a speeding car at the age of 74. He was cremated. That was his end of the business when he was with Pogue & Belmont, you know—the crematorium."

"That struck me as unusual. It was my impression that cremation is frowned on in Judaism."

She nodded. "Unusual, certainly. But not impossible, obviously. Jewish funeral practices vary."

"How fortunate that his cause of death is not in question, given that there is no body to post-mortem." Only Mac would think of that, and then say it to one of the dearly departed's family! "Witness aside, was there any reason for suspicion on your part that Mr. Brown deliberately ended his own life by stepping in front of that automobile?"

She took a deep breath. "To tell you the truth, I'm almost sure of it."

Mac raised an eyebrow. "Please elucidate."

"If you're looking for facts, Professor McCabe, I don't have any. It's just a feeling, and I know that feelings can be unreliable. But I could tell that Ira was depressed and drinking too much in the last few months of his life. That's not so unusual among the elderly, but I sensed that he was regretful about something he'd done, or maybe not done. No, it was more than that. He actually said more than once 'all my fault.' But he didn't say what. I asked him repeatedly, thinking maybe I could give him some peace of mind about whatever it was, but he just shook his head. Except once he said something like 'I don't deserve the money.' I think that's what it was, but he wouldn't repeat it when I asked him to. Ira was financially comfortable and lived in a nice house, but he wasn't rich."

"Was there anything else?"

She gave it some thought before saying, "One time he said something about 'a partnership made in hell.'"

Somebody had to ask the obvious, and I nominated me. "Was he talking about Pogue & Belmont, the funeral home business?"

"He didn't say, and I don't know much about that. It's ancient history—the three partners sold out to Jonathan Hawes's father long before I met Howard. Back then—1990—Ira was about the age I am now." That would be early 40s, I estimated, the same as her late husband.

"How did he refer to his former partners?" Mac wondered.

"He didn't. Not around me, anyway."

"You had no idea, then, that he was involved in a kind of insurance tontine with his former partners?"

Her face was a question mark. "What's that?"

"They insured each other," I explained. "Your father-in-law would have been paid a total of two million dollars if he'd outlived both his former partners, which seemed likely since he was the youngest—twelve years younger than Belmont and eighteen years younger than Pogue." I'd done the math earlier, not on the spot.

Sarah Fink-Brown's lovely hazel eyes grew large. "I had no idea."

Mac summarized: "Your father-in-law appeared haunted by something for which he took responsibility, possibly but not definitively related to his former involvement in the funeral home and cremation business, and you believe that it may have led him to end his own life in a particularly horrendous way."

She nodded.

"I'm just glad that Rabbi Goldman was with him at the end," she said. "Maybe that brought him some peace."

"WHY ARE WE going down this rabbit hole?" I asked Mac back in the gas guzzler.

"Because, old boy, it may have a rabbit in it."

I thought that's what magician's top hats are for.

He continued, looking thoughtful and forgetting to light a cigar: "I cannot shake the notion that those life insurance policies imply something stronger than the bonds of friendship forged among three men in business together more than three decades ago. It is common to have partner insurance, of course, but why maintain it decades later? Mr. Belmont's answer was unconvincing. And what of Ira Brown's assertion that he did not deserve the money? Surely that must have referred to—"

Mac's cell rang. Since we were still parked, I didn't have to endure the trauma of Sebastian McCabe's distracted driving.

"Yes, Johanna?"

He put her on speaker.

"Hi, Mac. I've been tasked with writing the mandatory below-the-fold Sunday feature story about the Pogue murder investigation, so I've got to pull something out of thin air." *Like a magician!* "So, what can you tell me to please my boss and enlighten our readers?"

As an *Observer* reader I would have questioned her priorities, but Mac said:

"I am not sure that pleasing Mr. Silverstein is within my skill set, although our relations have always been amicable."

"You know what I mean—how's your investigation going?"

"Investigation?" he bandied back. "Why do you presume my involvement in this sad business?"

"Oh, come on! Other than the fact that you've been involved in every other major crime in Erin since I got to town, and that you were in the Chief's office when I popped in, I'd say the fact that the victim was your friend and mentor—not to mention the fact that he left you a magician's trunk which someone, probably the killer, then stole—is a good reason."

Mac sighed and tried another tack at obfuscation:

"I have scarcely had time to begin any inquiries that Chief Hummel might find helpful. Dr. Eppensteiner only ruled Septimus's death a homicide yesterday."

A fact, but a misleading one.

"By which time it was old news to you," Johanna reminded Mac, "so don't be so coy. What have you been up to? Just between you and me and the readers of the *Observer*."

Cute. Let's see: We had Oscar's troops check alibis and see if any familiar names showed up on the Elysian Gardens sign-in sheet on the fateful day, while we talked to Wes Collier, Clay Belmont, Sarah Fink-Brown, and the three surviving members of the Pogue family. Never mind my sideshow with Ray Palmer at Balls & Strikes.

"At this point I am casting a wide net and all possibilities remain open. I prefer not to say more lest any comment of mine lead to misinterpretation."

Tall Rawls's frustration almost came through Mac's cell and yanked his beard. "If you missed a cliché there, I don't know what it was. Since you've handed me an empty sandwich, do you have any ideas what I can write about this case? Come on, Mac. I'm under the gun here, with just today and tomorrow to write a Sunday feature."

"Doubtless you have inquired of Chief Hummel—"

"'Our investigation is ongoing,'" she quoted. "I'm not any more satisfied with that than Adrian Pogue is."

"Adrian Pogue?" Mac repeated.

"He called me, royally pissed at what he sees as lack of action in his father's murder. I think he called the mayor's office, too. He's worth a quote or two, but I'm not going to build a whole story around his impatience."

"You could interview Lexi Pogue aka Alakazandra the magician," I suggested, channeling my journalistic instincts. "She would make a great feature story, 'Magician copes with murder of grandfather role model' or some such, filled in with a few meaningless quotes from Mac and Oscar."

From the driver's seat, Mac raised an eyebrow at me and pulled out a cigar.

"That's actually not a bad idea, Jeff," Tall Rawls allowed.

"Don't sound so surprised."

"I guess Lexi's not a suspect, huh?"

"More like a client," I said. "If we had clients."

Good newsperson that she is, Johanna didn't stop there. But Mac, between puffs on the Antonio de la Cova, artfully dodged her questions about whether the other Pogues or Lafcadio Figg were under his magnifying glass. Clay Belmont apparently wasn't on her radar, given that his name didn't come up.

"Well," she sighed at last, "at least you've given me an angle."

"Glad to help," I told her.

WE MET WITH Rabbi David Goldman in his handsome study at Congregation Beth Israel. He's a cuddly bear of a man approaching his mid-sixties, with curly light brown hair. Mac and I know him best as one of three clerical tenors in the group A Joyful Noise and an adjunct professor of Hebrew Scripture at SBU. We sat in a pair of comfortable padded leather chairs, while the rabbi remained at his mahogany desk.

He agreed to speak with us about his late congregant, but with some reluctance.

"I am not bound as a priest is by the seal of the confessional, of course, but nevertheless . . ."

"We would not wish you to share any confidence in a way that violates a trust," Mac assured him. "However, we are dealing with a murder."

"Surely not in the death of Ira Brown?"

"Surely not," Mac agreed. "At least, not as the term is usually understood. There seems to be no reason to doubt the assumption that your congregant was struck by a hit-and-run driver in a tragic accident. However, in all candor, the suggestion has been made that Mr. Brown engineered his own death—suicide by auto, one might say."

Rabbi Goldman folded his hands across his girth. "In equal candor, I cannot say that surprises me. When I arrived at St. Hildegarde, he was very near death and clearly not easy in his conscience. Or so it seemed to me. Perhaps I am projecting, but he was quite agitated and kept mumbling what sounded to me like 'red markets.'"

Red! I was suddenly hit by what Mac might call a frisson and I call the creepy-crawlies. The year before we'd been wrapped up in a case where that color was everywhere.[13]

---

[13] See *The Woman in Red* (MX Publishing, 2023).

"I looked up the phrase online and found a meaning that surprised me."

"The illegal sale of human organs?" Mac said.

"What? Good heavens, no. 'Red Markets' is the name of a tabletop role-playing game about cut-throat—literally cut-throat—competition amidst the economic horror that follows a zombie apocalypse."

Mac's eyebrows shot up. "How extraordinary!"

"I'll say," I piled on. "Wouldn't an old man be more likely to play cribbage or something?" Whatever cribbage is.

"Ira was not an old man," Rabbi Goldman said. "He was 74. Also, he was a science fiction fan and a member of Sister Mary Margaret Malone's science fiction book club at Mo's Mysteries and Marvels bookstore. Perhaps he heard about the game from a younger friend." I made a mental note to ask Triple M about that. My mental file cabinet was starting to get almost as cluttered as Mac's office.

"Still," Mac said, "it is an odd thing for a man to have on his mind in his last hours."

The rabbi leaned forward. "Maybe not. Maybe it was an indication of his depressed state of mind, stemming from an economic horror of his own."

"If so, his daughter-in-law was unaware of it. She referred to his financial circumstances as 'comfortable.'"

The rabbi gave what a novelist might call a wan smile. "In my experience, Professor McCabe, it is not at all unusual for close family members of a deceased to learn things about that person of which they had no suspicion. The human being is a mystery that even you cannot solve."

Chapter Twelve
Ghouls

BREAKFAST TIME AT the Cody house the next morning, Saturday, with Lynda hunched over the *Wall Street Journal* crossword puzzle while the Cody kids dug into their corn flakes:

"Number 69 across. What's a word for retirement plan, darling?"

"IRA? 401K?"

"No, it's five letters. Oh, there's a question mark at the end—that means it's not serious. And the last letter is P. SLEEP! That's not my retirement plan, but I get it. Here's another five-letter word. 'Charming person?'"

"WITCH," I said.

"That's it!"

So, thoughts of city council candidate and witch Zoraida Quant dodged in and out of my brain as I loaded the dishwasher after breakfast. As one of nine council members she couldn't do that much damage—unless, of course, she hexed something. Maybe I was too hasty in dismissing her ability to do that. But these musings were soon interrupted by an early-morning call from Mac.

"Alexandra would like us to update her in person on our progress," he informed me.

"We haven't made any."

"Nonsense, Jefferson! It is quite likely that we know what we need to know. The only problem is that we do not yet know that we know it."

"That's easy for you to say, but I'm not sure it's going to thrill the magic lady."

SHE ASKED US to meet her at her grandfather's house. It was about twice the size of her own, built in the storybook style that was popular on the West Coast in the early 1920s and 1930s. My dad, the real estate broker, loves that design—half-timbering, multiple rooflines and gables, and a turret. It struck me that Pogue did okay for himself despite the embezzlement by what's-his-name, the guy who did a vanishing act and cost the three partners their funeral home business.

When Lexi opened the door, dressed in a cream-colored blouse and black slacks that made her seem even taller, she was talking on the phone just as she had been during our midweek visit. A lot had happened since then, although Mac's doubletalk hadn't convinced me we'd made any progress along the way.

"I'll be sure to keep you in mind," the magician/wedding planner said, rolling her eyes as she waved us in. "But don't call me again, I'll call you."

She disconnected, adding "like hell I will!" as we all sat down in the living room. And for our benefit she threw in, "More ghouls!"

The word—the same appellation she'd applied to Logan Drake and Lafcadio Figg at her grandfather's memorial service—seemed kind of appropriate with Halloween three days away, but I didn't say so.

"Magic memorabilia collectors?" Mac speculated.

"Right. I've heard from half a dozen so far, including Logan Drake. I'm like, 'Quit circling, you sharks.'" She was mixing metaphors, ghouls and sharks, but she was upset. "They contacted my father, the next of kin listed in the obit, who passed them on to me because I inherited the lot. If the collection had gone to Dad, he would have sold out to the highest bidder the day after the funeral, if he waited that long. But I'm not ready to let go yet; that collection meant so much to Granddad."

Lexi sighed. "I suppose I'll have to sell most of it eventually, though. If the early offers are any indication, I won't be able to refuse. That kind of money is too good to pass up for somebody who isn't exactly rich. And I'm not a collector; that was Granddad's thing."

"You have my empathy for the hounding you have endured," Mac said. "I myself have received communications from a number of individuals eager to purchase the Blackstone trunk and the contents—including a man who offered to take Septimus's baseball cards off my hands." That would be Ray Palmer of Balls & Strikes, whose name I had been careful not to utter in Mac's presence. He didn't need to know about my unsuccessful side venture in sleuthing. "I confess that those pieces of cardboard do not have for me the emotional resonance of Harry Houdini's handcuffs or Professor Carlo Stuarti's Victorian-era crystal ball. In fact, I suspect that their presence in the trunk was a mere happenstance and not an intentional gift for me. Nevertheless, I have informed all inquirers that I have no intention of disposing of anything in the trunk until Septimus's killer is identified, tried, and punished—if then."

"So where are you with the first part—finding out who killed Granddad? I hope it's one of the collectors."

"Alas, Mr. Drake seems practically eliminated by virtue of the tight time frame between his nightly performance at the Forty Thieves Casino and Septimus's death. And the team of Tinker & Skyles performed that day in Las Vegas." Mac paused. "Someone less imaginative than I would point to Septimus's heirs as the most obvious beneficiaries from his death."

I had the distinct impression it was a good thing Lexi didn't have a cup of super-hot coffee in her hand suitable for throwing in Mac's face. "That's absurd!"

"Your Aunt Sable was a familiar fixture at Elysian Gardens," Mac noted mildly.

"What? That's crazy! She was Granddad's greatest advocate with Elysian over his treatment there. She loved him. You can't fake that."

I expected Mac to respond by calling that "a dubious assertion" or some such. Instead, he pivoted.

"Your father, on the other hand, had no such warm relations with *his* father."

After a while, perhaps pondering that, Lexi said, "I think Dad loved Granddad, too, in his own weird way; that's why he was so hurt by Granddad's lack of faith in his crazy schemes. And if you're thinking of a money motive, I'm sure Dad was shocked that he inherited."

"He certainly appeared to be so when I informed him," Mac allowed.

"If your aunt and your father loved Septimus Pogue so much, maybe one of them decided to put him out of his pain," I suggested.

"You mean, like, euthanasia? They don't believe in that. Besides, Dad never went to the nursing home."

"That you know of," I countered. "Maybe he went there in disguise and signed in under another name." The possibility of *somebody* doing that was always on the table.

Lexi rolled her blue eyes, a reaction I have been known to provoke from my spouse. "Maybe I was expecting too much. I thought the great Sebastian McCabe and sidekick would do more than just speculate."

Sidekick! That stung, but Mac appeared unruffled by this not-so-subtle critique.

"Jefferson and I have not been lacking in energy, Miss Pogue. We have spoken with a number of relevant *dramatis personae* in this little drama, including your father and your mother. She visited Septimus the day he died."

"Stepmother," Lexi corrected. "Cindy LeVan is my stepmother. Not a bad sort, really, and still seems to love my father, even though she can't live with him—no surprise there. But she's not my mother. Mom died ten years ago. Anyway, what else?"

"More importantly, perhaps, we have spoken with Septimus's surviving partner, Clayton Belmont, and with the daughter-in-law of their third partner, Ira Brown. I am convinced that something other than business and fellowship bound those 'blood brothers' together. What that something is, and how it relates to the murder, is what we need to ferret out."

"Just find out who killed Granddad. Please."

"AT LEAST SHE can't fire us—she's not paying us," I told Mac as she closed the door.

"That is cold comfort indeed, Jefferson. You saw the look of disappointment on her face."

Resisting the temptation to enjoy this rare moment of McCabe self-doubt, I assured him, "You'll solve it."

"I appreciate your confidence, old boy. Let us hope that our interview with Dr. Abington will be a step in that direction."

"Abington?"

"Did I neglect to mention that we also have an appointment with him this morning?"

"I was planning to cut the grass."

"Surely it will not grow to a significant degree if that chore is postponed by a few hours?"

It wound up being a little longer than that.

We caught up with Dr. Thomas Abington taking in a girls' volleyball game at Bernardin High School. His younger daughter, Ruth, was on the team.

"Thank you for agreeing to meet with us, Doctor," Mac said.

"Do you still smoke cigars?" Abington wanted to know.

Almost at a loss for words, Mac said simply, "I do."

"Don't kid yourself: They aren't benign just because they aren't cigarettes."

Said the doctor who was at least forty pounds overweight, with closely cropped graying hair. He was about fifty and handsome, according to Lynda.

"Be that as it may, can you confirm for us that Septimus was about to be put into hospice care when he died?"

"I'm not sure it would be ethical for me to comment on that."

"Would you answer the question if put by Chief Hummel or one of his officers?"

"Atta girl, Ruth! Way to serve!" Then to Mac he said: "Yeah, I guess so."

"Well, they aren't here," I said, "but if we weren't, one of them might be."

"I think I get your point. You aren't just asking out of curiosity, and I'd rather talk to you than Oscar Hummel or one of his cops. Yes, Septimus Pogue was dying of advanced pancreatic cancer and my advice was to move him to a place where he could be more comfortable until the end. It was a matter of weeks at the most. I thought the idea of an autopsy was ridiculous until I found the fentanyl."

"You performed the post-mortem yourself in your capacity as an assistant coroner?"

A blink. "That's right. It wasn't the first time I'd done that for a friend and patient. A final service, in a way. You have to get used to it in a county this size if you want to work for the coroner, even as a side gig."

"How do you think the drug was administered?"

"Probably through the line." Mac had suggested as much earlier. "That wouldn't be difficult, even for a non-medical type. Just inject it."

"And you visited Septimus the day he died."

A nod. "Right again."

"What can you tell us about that visit?"

A shrug. "Not much. He knew what was ahead and seemed resigned to it. He wasn't in a lot of pain."

"Why did you visit if there was nothing you could do for him?"

"Septimus didn't get many visitors." After a pause, Abington added: "I'd known him for a long time. I drove a hearse for Pogue & Belmont that last summer they were in business—before I went off to university. I'm Clay Belmont's

PCP, too." *That's Primary Care Physician for you civilians—what was once known as a GP.*

"I guess you would have known Ira Brown, too," I said.

It would be too much to say that Abington shuddered, but the memory of Brown's body run over by a car clearly wasn't a pleasant one. "That's right, although I wasn't his PCP. I did that PM, too."

"Do you find it an odd coincidence that the two former partners died in such close proximity?" Mac asked.

"I don't find it a coincidence at all, McCabe. People die every day. And the circumstances were totally different. Shake it off, Ruth!"

INSTEAD OF HAVING lunch at home with my beloved spouse and adorable trio of offspring, my empty stomach and I found ourselves at noon in the room of Mac's house on Half Moon Street that he calls his study and everybody else knows is a man cave. We were watching a video of Logan Drake on the big-screen TV above the bar—Mac from behind his desk and I from a comfortable chair in a corner next to the fireplace. On the screen the devilish-looking magician made a square birdcage disappear from his hands, with a bird inside, then did the same repeatedly with members of the audience holding the cage.

"A classic Harry Blackstone illusion," Mac observed at the end. "Both Blackstones, *père* and *fils*, performed it to great success."

"Good to know. But why are we watching this less-than-blockbuster venture into streamed magic?"

Mac had been unusually silent while driving away from the high school gym, then insisted that we decamp to the Mac Cave, where he poured me a Caffeine-Free Diet Coke from the tap on his bar (too early for beer for me) and started streaming *The Magical World of Logan Drake*. The eponymous star of the series, which ran for six episodes on Hulu in 2019, had less gray hair in his temples on the show but just as much oiliness in his patter.

"Logan Drake has been quite persistent in his pursuit of the Septimus Pogue magic collection," Mac replied.

"Collectors are always persistent."

Not to mention strange.

"Fair point, old boy! At any rate, he has caught my attention."

"You mean he's the straw you're grasping at, at the moment."

Mac ignored this statement of the obvious. "I knew him peripherally when he was a boy. I am trying to get a measure of the man."

"Does it bother you that he could be Damon Devlin come to life?"

"He? Nonsense! Any resemblance to my protagonist is purely superficial—they are both magicians who sport beards of a Luciferine shape, in the manner of both Septimus Pogue and Blackstone Senior's contemporary Dante the Magician, who was really a Dane named Jansen."

We're really getting into the weeds here, with no gardener in sight.

"You're the one who said it was 'implausible' that Drake could have killed Pogue and made it to his performance at the casino on time," I pointed out.

"And I believe you are the one who uttered the term 'hit man' with regard to Tinker & Skyles."

"Well, you have me there. He could have outsourced his dirty work. And there is the Blackstone connection—Drake does Blackstone's tricks, Blackstone's trunk was stolen. But wait! How do you explain the trunk turning up at Lyceum? It's not like Drake the Murderous Magician would have stuck it there. He had no reason to."

"Well, that is a puzzler, to be sure. And that is only one of the vexing conundrums that we face. There remains, for example, the intriguing question of why Ira Brown sought his own self-destruction—if he indeed did—and what united the three former partners."

While Mac drummed his fingers on his desk, I moved on.

"Let's stick with magicians for a minute. I like Lexi, alias Alaka-whozzits, but she has a Class A motive to kill her beloved grandfather. She's being hounded by collectors to buy the magical gizmos and whatnots that she inherited. That means the prices offered are going to go through the roof—simple supply and demand. And she even admitted she'll eventually sell most of it. And Septimus Pogue was dying anyway, so the fentanyl only speeded up the process a little, and painlessly at that."

At this point I was running out of breath.

"Ah, the old client as killer trope!" Mac said. "That even happened to Sherlock Holmes on more than one occasion. However, I fear there is a slight flaw in your reasoning, Jefferson. If the motive was inheritance, no murder was necessary. Septimus was just weeks from natural death, according to Dr. Abington."

I had no answer to that, but thinking of Lexi Pogue had sent the Cody brain off in another direction.

"Lexi changed the subject very quickly when the topic of her mother came up. What's that all about?"

"I know almost nothing about Septimus's family, obviously including Alexandra's mother. Perhaps she—"

Mac's phone rang.

"Sebastian McCabe here!"

He didn't put the call on speaker, but he didn't need to. The voice at the other end came through loud and clear.

"This is Roger Belmont. Have you been to lunch yet?"

Mac raised an eyebrow. "Hello, Mr. Belmont. I am here with my friend Thomas Jefferson Cody, and no, I have not."

"Please meet me, both of you, at Malarkey's Pub in half an hour. I do a lot of business over meals there."

"Oh, do we have business?"

"I think so."

Chapter Thirteen

The Candidates

MALARKEY'S IS RIGHT off the lobby of the Winfield Hotel, less formal than the hotel's Mimosa restaurant but a few cuts above eating trail mix at my desk or even lunching at Daniel's Apothecary (décor and menu 1950s malt shop).

Arriving first, we spent some time gawking at the classic lines of the 1931 Winfield lobby.

"Do you think this is a tactic—making us wait?" I asked after about five minutes, part of which I spent exchanging romantic text messages with Lynda just to keep the fire burning until I could get home.

"You have developed a devious mind, Jefferson."

"Thanks, but you're the mystery writer." I'd abandoned my efforts in that direction about a dozen years ago in favor of these true crime accounts of Sebastian McCabe.

Not long after this witty repartee I spotted Roger Belmont shuffling our way, decked out in a 3½-inch Tom Ford silk tie ($270), a navy suit, loafers, and a Rolex Submariner watch that I'm pretty sure cost more than my New Beetle Final Edition. "Littlejohn for the Little Guys," as his company's slogan had it, seemed lucrative for this particular small-town financial advisor.

Belmont was all smiles and handshakes. "Thanks for meeting me." But ten minutes later, after a bouncy young server with a ring in her nose had deposited the menus and I was trying to decide between tuna salad and grilled cheese with tomato soup, Belmont said:

"I've got a bone to pick with you, McCabe."

I turned my head to see Mac, who was sitting next to me and across the table from our host, lift an eyebrow. "How so?"

"You got my father all worked up by asking him about that Pogue murder business, practically accused him of being involved."

"I assure you, Mr. Belmont—"

"I mean, what the hell are you thinking?" His square face turned reddish and the eyes behind his glasses looked a little wild. "Septimus Pogue and my father were old friends."

"Indeed," said Mac, "so much so that they named each other as beneficiaries of insurance policies."

"What?" He dropped the menu that he wasn't looking at. "That's news to me."

Then if you were his financial advisor, you weren't a very good one. Or your father was hiding it from you.

"It was a sort of tontine among the former partners of the long-closed funeral home business," Mac explained. "Your father was also the contingent beneficiary of a policy that would have gone to their third partner, Ira Brown, had he not died."

If I'd just been given that news, I would have asked how much the policies were for—but then, I wasn't wearing a Rolex. Belmont just shook his head and said, "I had no idea. I hope it wasn't whole life insurance. It's much better to buy term insurance and invest the difference." Since I agreed, I revised my opinion about his prowess as a financial advisor while he went on. "Don't tell me you think an 86-year-old man killed an old friend, a nursing home resident, for some insurance money? My father's in great health, but even if he lives to be a hundred . . . This is lunacy, McCabe."

He shut up then as our server came back with our drinks to take orders. I went for the tuna salad while my tablemates opted for heart attack specials.

"You are disputing an assertion I have not made," Mac told Belmont when we were alone again. "I am merely gathering facts."

"Butting into a police investigation," Belmont translated.

"At Chief Hummel's request."

"I'm not impressed by him. He hasn't done anything about all the electric scooter accidents in this town. Public safety is one of my passions, and I expect to be on that committee when I'm elected to city council next month. Don't forget to vote, by the way. And I'll also be taking a close look at Hummel's performance review. That assistant chief of his, Gibbons, he'd make a good chief."

Well, that's true.

"But back to the subject at hand, if you have to butt in, McCabe, you should be taking a close look at Pogue's own family. They had the easiest access to him and I'm sure they inherit."

"You know the family?"

"Some of them. Sable's okay—she's a client of mine. I saw Lexi perform at a private party once, and I thought she was a pretty good magician. But doesn't that mean she's an expert at deception? Adrian I've never met, although I know he's a lunatic. No wonder his wife killed herself."

"What!" That must have been me because Mac doesn't know any words with only one syllable.

"Didn't you know? Well, it wasn't exactly part of her obituary notice, but I thought somebody would have mentioned it to you. Elle Pogue, who was Lexi's mother, took an overdose of sleeping pills."

"WELL, ADRIAN DOES seem to be a bit of a stormy petrel of untimely demises," Mac mused later as he drove me home in his big red machine. "His father was murdered a decade after his wife killed herself."

"If she did kill herself," I said. "Two suicides in the orbit of Adrian Pogue—Ira Brown being the other—seem suspicious to me."

"Sometimes a cigar is just a cigar, as Freud probably did not say."

"What does your odious habit have to do with anything?"

"It is not a habit; it is an indulgence. My point is that there may be nothing especially meaningful about two suicides in a decade, especially since one was only marginally related to Adrian Pogue through his estranged father. How many people do you know who have taken their own life?"

I gave that a think, taking me back to my boyhood in Virginia. "Three," I admitted.

"Well, there you have it."

He pulled out a cigar.

AFTER DINNER THAT evening, the last Saturday before Halloween, Lynda and I and Sister Mary Margaret Malone took the kids (Triple M calls them "the Munchkins") to the House of Fear. This was the fourth year for that corny haunted house benefiting the Kiwanis Club of Erin. It had been organized by Lafcadio Figg, named for an old Sherlock Holmes movie starring Basil Rathbone, and involved many of the actors from the Lyceum Players. Jonathan Hawes, for example, lay in one of his own coffins—until he sat up and scared the living crap out of the younger and/or more excitable patrons.

"Rabbi Goldman told us that Ira Brown was a member of your science fiction book club," I informed Triple M as we were waiting to get in.

"Yeah," she said. "I miss him. He was a sweet guy."

If anybody should know sweet, it would be Triple M, who defines the term. She's also cute, with her short dark hair parted in the middle, and looks much younger than her 40-plus years. Also, the woman has been known to use holy cards for bookmarks in horror novels.

"Was he into zombies?" I asked, thinking of the "Red Markets" game that seemed to explain the mumbled words the rabbi overheard.

"Not that I know of. Ira liked fantasy—he was a huge *Lord of the Rings* fan. Oh, look, there's Mo!"

Mo Russert, wife of Jonathan Hawes and co-owner of Mo's Mysteries and Marvels (along with supposedly silent partner Sebastian McCabe), was dressed as a witch and stirring a large cauldron outside the haunted house, formerly a small school building.

"That explains the picket."

Marching back and forth on the sidewalk was a lonely protestor holding the hand-painted sign "Unfair to Witches." It was Zoraida Quant.

PILLOW TALK AT the Cody house that night:

"I saw two city council candidates today and they both scared me," I told Lynda.

"I believe you. I still like my theory that Quant killed Pogue for what she considered to be mocking magic by pretending to perform it—kind of like sacrilege, as she saw it—whether or not the trunk had anything to do with it."

"But there must be hundreds of thousands of magicians pretending to do magic!"

"Not in Erin."

"Well, true enough, but Pogue's granddaughter is in Erin and she performs for audiences, which Septimus didn't do anymore. Shouldn't that make her even more kill-worthy than him?"

"Maybe so, but we're not near the end of the book. Isn't there usually at least one more murder? Lexi could be in danger!"

I couldn't argue with that, so I said: "You ought to be writing fiction."

"I do, darling."

"Oh, right. But those are family sagas, not mysteries."

"Call Mac tomorrow and see what he thinks."

Chapter Fourteen
Or Was It Murder?

SUNDAY MORNING PHONE call, after church:

MAC: "In addition to the objection you raised to Lynda's theory, there is the question of why Ms. Quant would kill an individual who is dying in a nursing home and largely forgotten except by family and close friends."

JEFF: "Number one, revenge. Number two, Zoraida Quant isn't playing with a full deck of Tarot cards. I'm just playing devil's advocate here."

MAC: "I remain curious about Elle Pogue's presumed suicide."

JEFF: "You mean you're suspicious?"

MAC: "I am always suspicious."

JEFF: "That's a quotable quote, but not literally true—and I never use the overused word 'literally.'"

MAC: "You just did, old boy."

JEFF: "Anyway, what could Elle Pogue's death have to do with the murder of her father-in-law ten years later?"

MAC: "That remains to be seen. Perhaps the answer to that question formerly resided in the magician's trunk. Remember, there is no reason to assume that the contents of that trunk are complete as Septimus left them."

And so on.

Mac lauded the feature story taking up prime real estate on the front page of the Sunday *Observer & News-Ledger,* with a nice photo of the bald and beautiful Lexi Pogue in a colorful caftan under the headline: **MAGICIAN CARRIES ON POGUE MAGICAL TRADITION**.

"An excellent specimen of Johanna's skills in both writing and reportage," he proclaimed it.

Running 30 inches of type beneath the Rawls byline, the story focused on the subject's relationship with her murdered grandfather, the investigation of said murder being a side issue. Johanna also made a passing mention of Lexi's inheritance of the Septimus Pogue collection of stage magic. Here's a representative sampling of the piece:

> "I was always sorry that the Lords of Legerdemain were dissolved by the time I showed up," Pogue said. "I would have loved to have learned the magical arts as part of a community. But I had my granddad. That was enough."
>
> The favorite trick he taught her is one in which she holds up a deck of cards in a glass. Members of the audience, whether at a wedding or a children's party, think of a card without telling which one out loud. That card then rises from the deck.
>
> "Kids love that one," Pogue said. "Granddad used to do it with baseball cards when he performed himself, before he went into the funeral business."
>
> The prestidigitator notes that female magicians have been successful for well over a century, with some major examples being Adelaide

Herrmann, "the Queen of Magic"; Mercedes Talma, "the Queen of Coins"; Ionia, "the Goddess of Mystery"; Anna Eva Fay, "the High Priestess of Mystery"; and Susy Wandas, "the Lady with Fairy Fingers, the Paganini of the Cards, and the Virtuoso of the Cigarettes."

As Alakazandra, Pogue makes a striking figure. Does she herself envision someday performing on a bigger stage than Erin?

"Maybe," she says, "when I get good enough. But I haven't given that a lot of thought lately. The number one thing on my mind right now is seeing Granddad's killer brought to justice. I won't rest until that happens."

The story didn't mention her father, nor the suicide of her mother.

"Perhaps Frank Woodford could shed some light on the late Mrs. Pogue," Mac said. "He appears to know all the news that is not fit to print."

"ELLE POGUE?" THE *Observer*'s "To Be Frank" columnist repeated when Mac reached him on a conference call Monday morning. "That's going back aways, but I remember. I was a reporter then." I could hear nostalgia in his voice. "We didn't write about it, of course. It was a family tragedy."

"What happened?"

"Classic suicide which the family preferred to think was an accident: She took an overdose of sleeping pills."

No wonder Lexi didn't want to talk about it. But maybe there was another reason. "Did her daughter find the body?" I asked.

"No, her next-door neighbor and good friend found her outside on the patio. It was a fine spring day and Elle had washed the pills down with coffee. I remember that because the neighbor's husband, Art LeVan, was a hell of a golfer who dropped dead on the seventh hole. That's the way I'd like to go myself."

"LeVan?" Mac repeated. "Was he perhaps the brother of Cindy LeVan?"

"Husband. It was Cindy who found the body."

After he disconnected, Mac stayed on the line—each of us in our own offices—and I summarized the situation:

"So, Adrian Pogue's second wife found his first wife's body, dead of an apparent suicide, while she herself was married to another man, who later died of an apparent heart attack while playing golf. Nothing suspicious there at all." Call that sarcastic if you must. I prefer to think of it as ironic.

"You posit that Adrian Pogue has acquired a habit of homicide?"

"A man who reads animals' minds and lives in a flying saucer is capable of anything."

"Perhaps we should visit Ms. LeVan."

After the usual protestations that I had work to do— somewhat undercut by the hovering Popcorn's snort that I'm pretty sure was audible to Mac—I agreed to go with him, but later.

CINDY LEVAN WAS a hairdresser with a chair at Myrtle White's Glam Gurlz beauty salon on College Street, where Lynda has her honey-blonde curls (the real thing!) trimmed and set monthly. After lunch at my desk and a huddle with Sylvester Link about developing some new features for *Ben*, Mac and I met her there in the back room. She agreed to give us half an hour, and I had the strong feeling she would be keeping a close eye on her smartwatch.

"Adrian may have been estranged from his father, but that doesn't mean he wasn't devastated by this murder business," she assured us, gripping a cup of coffee.

This didn't seem the time to tell her that double negatives are confusing.

"You appear to be remarkably supportive of your former spouse," Mac observed.

LeVan smiled. "I love the guy; I just can't live with him. He's too—what shall I say?"

Try "mad as a hatter."

She settled on, "Unrooted in reality, off in la-la land, loony as a loon." *In other words, mad as a hatter.* "On top of that, I just couldn't take the economic insecurity. He was spending my money as well as his on his crazy ideas. So, we got a divorce three years ago and he moved into that goofy house. I drop by once in a while to make sure he doesn't forget to eat. And sometimes I rip his clothes off of him and wash them."

"Speaking of money," I said, "Adrian inherited some from his father."

"It would be nice to say he feels guilty about that, but I'm afraid Adrian isn't that self-aware. But he is just gutted that Septimus was murdered."

She either missed my point that Adrian was the *cui* in the old *cui bono* question, or she wanted us to think she did.

"I gather that you originally knew him as a next-door neighbor," Mac said.

The expression on her round face was not a happy one. "What's that got to do with anything?"

"It was merely an observation."

"Adrian is a sweet man who gave our dog Sherwood grief counseling after Art died. I really didn't know him well until then. He was just my friend's husband."

"That friend being Elle Pogue. And you found her body, did you not?"

Mac was clearly taking Cindy LeVan where she didn't want to go. "That was a couple of years before Art died," she snapped. "Look, this is all history. Bad history. I don't want to talk about it anymore. And I have to get back to work. I don't get paid to sit around and talk."

Neither do I, but that doesn't stop me.

LeVan stood up and exited the back room. Mac and I followed her out, nodding to the always-upbeat Myrtle White on our way through the salon. She responded with a big smile and wished us a blessed day.

"Well, Jefferson, what do you think of your theory now?" Mac asked when we were back in the Macmobile.

"I think it's interesting that Cindy LeVan doesn't want to talk about her friend's alleged suicide and was so quick to let us know that she barely knew Adrian when it happened."

"You, sir, have developed a devious mind."

"It's the company I keep."

Mac consulted his left wrist, which is decorated with a Sherlock Holmes watch. (I haven't worn a watch since Mac removed mine during a magic trick without me noticing.) "It is rather late in the day to return to campus. I propose that we pay a call on Alexandra and see if we can get her to be more forthcoming on the subject of her mother."

"Again? She wasn't exactly thrilled with us when we left her on Saturday."

"It is not our task to be popular."

"Good thing."

I scanned my e-mail, texts, and social media as Mac drove. Lynda informed me that we were having spaghetti for dinner, Popcorn noted that Morrie Kindle's story about the Stop the Lies in the Skies group's protest of Dr. Lamplighter's talk had gone out on the AP wire, and Riley St. Simon was flooding Instagram with photos of the new Bainbridge Building under construction.

When I looked up again, we were approaching Lexi Pogue's house and a familiar figure was coming out the front door. Said door slammed behind him.

"Isn't that Logan Drake, whom we last heard being given the brush-off by Lexi via phone?" I asked Mac. It was a rhetorical question.

"Indeed! The man is nothing if not persistent."

We exited the Chevy and headed toward Lexi's A-frame. Drake, coming down the front walk, saw us and affixed a smile that didn't reach his eyes. He stopped and we caught up to him. Although I felt as though I knew Drake from seeing him perform at the funeral and on videos, we'd never been introduced. Mac performed that chore, which was followed by the handshake ritual.

"Comforting the bereaved?" Mac asked him.

Drake had the good taste to look slightly embarrassed. "That would be stretching it. I'm a collector of magic memorabilia, and Lexi just inherited a crapload of it. Connect the dots."

"I already have. And the result of your efforts?"

"No joy. She's playing hard to get because she knows there will be other bidders and she wants to get the best price."

"There is one other possibility."

The magician looked puzzled. "And that is?"

"That sentiment for her grandfather makes her loath at this point in the mourning process to part with the collection that was so much a part of him."

"Maybe, but in my experience, sentiment usually has a price." Drake paused. "Speaking of which, how much do you want for Blackstone's trunk?"

Mac's self-control was impressive. He merely said: "I would impoverish myself before I would sell it."

Drake hauled out the pro forma smile again, along with a white plastic card with a gold QR code on it. "I'll tell you what I told Lexi: When you're ready, just scan this into your phone for my contact info."

"When I am ready, I certainly shall."

Which will be about twelve minutes after hell freezes over, the look on Mac's face said.

"Well, this has been fun, gentlemen," Drake said, "but I have a performance to prepare for."

"What specifically did he want?" Mac asked Lexi.

She had a large glass of red wine in her hand when she opened the door. The black cat Houdini looked up at her accusingly from his position at her feet, but I had no such judgement. I might have been drinking, too, if Adrian Pogue was my father. Besides, it was almost five o'clock and maybe she was finished planning weddings and practicing magic for the day.

"Anything he could get his hands on," she answered Mac, "including me. I'm like, 'get lost,' but apparently that was too subtle. I finally told him to make like a magician and disappear before I called my boyfriend. What a slimeball. I wouldn't put anything past—Wait! Are you here to tell me he killed Granddad?"

She looked hopeful.

"Satisfying though that may be at some level," Mac said, "that is not the reason for our return. We wanted to speak with you about the painful subject of your mother's suicide."

Lexi stiffened, then drank. "Why? I mean, what could that possibly have anything to do with anything after all these years?"

"In my experience, Alexandra, the past can cast a long shadow," Mac said. "Your grandfather's former business partner Ira Brown seemed haunted by it, for example, and now he is dead—possibly of his own volition. That may be relevant to my old friend's demise, however. Something much simpler may be at play here. Did you ever suspect that your mother's death was not suicide?"

"What? Absolutely not! Mom struggled with mental illness for years. What she did was a tragedy, but not a surprise even to me as a nineteen-year-old college student. I don't see how—" She stopped, stunned. "You're wondering whether Dad killed her!"

"It has crossed my mind that your father's father and his first wife both died unnatural deaths. And, under Ohio law, he had to inherit at least half of his spouse's assets, and probably more if they had wills."

"Half of nothing is still nothing. Mom had less money than Dad. She came from a poor family and worked as a cashier at Home Depot."

"What about life insurance?" I asked.

"If Dad had any big money from an insurance settlement, he wouldn't have tried to get Granddad to stake him in his crackbrain schemes."

Actually, he'd had plenty of time to run through a pile since Elle Pogue's death, and thus need a cash refill, but Mac let that pass.

"Money is not the only possible motive for homicide," he pointed out. "Consider love and hate, for example."

Lexi finished her drink in a swallow and wandered into the kitchen to get a refill, talking all the while. "Dad's a fruitcake, but I never doubted that he loved my mom, or that he was shattered by her death. He was a basket case when he called me with the news. And I know he wasn't faking because he's terrible at lying. He could never be a magician."

"And yet he remarried."

"Three years later." Lexi poured what was left of a bottle of Cabernet Sauvignon, whether pricey or not I haven't a clue. "I won't say that didn't bother me at the time. But later I read that happily married people are more likely to re-marry after their spouses die because they had a good experience the first time. I do feel sorry for Cindy, though."

She drank, not daintily, then added:

"Hey, I meant to thank you for having that reporter call me, Jeff. The story came out pretty well, didn't it?"

"PERHAPS WE ARE seeing things that are not there, Jefferson," Mac mused as we drove away. "Most likely Elle Pogue's death was truly a suicide."

"So where does that leave us, other than up a creek without a canoe?"

"It leaves me continuing to wonder whether Ira Brown's death was truly suicide by auto or not, and what qualm of conscience so disturbed him as he lay dying."

Chapter Fifteen
Death on All Hallows' Eve

THERE THE POGUE case sat the next day while I was chained to my desk answering media inquiries, brainstorming with Popcorn, drafting a speech, and meeting with the efficient and effective Lesley Saylor-Mackie, who is my immediate boss in her dual roles of executive vice president and provost of St. Benignus University. Mac was presumably doing whatever tenured professors do, if anything, except for a brief call to relay Oscar's report that Clay Belmont's playing-poker-at-the-country-club alibi checked out and that Belmont was neither signed in at Elysian Gardens nor a familiar visage to staff.

That evening was chilly but clear—good weather for Halloween, which Mac insists on calling All Hallows' Eve.

"I'm Wonder Woman!" Donata announced, although the costume made that obvious even on a 7-year-old. Her 5-year-old brothers, Sam and Jake, appeared as Superman and Batman, respectively.

"Didn't we get enough superheroes in that 'woman in red' murder business last year?" I groused to Lynda, fetchingly garbed as Captain Marvel and filling out the costume to perfection.

"The world can never have too many superheroes, darling."

There are days when I long for just one.

Lynda took the Cody kids trick-or-treating with next-door neighbor Ginger Ronson-Patch and son Andy (dressed as a crayon). Aaron Patch and I gave out candy from the comfort of our chairs on the driveway, warmed by a portable fire pit. Princesses were still popular among all ages—and so were witches! That had me thinking about Zoraida Quant. Who knows what a woman like that was capable of? If she got elected to city council in exactly one week, we'd find out. The thought gave me chills despite the fire.

"Is McCabe wearing a deerstalker for Halloween?" Patch wanted to know as he cracked a beer.

"That wouldn't be a disguise."

Disguise! Who would be better at disguise than a stage magician? Logan Drake could have disguised himself, maybe as a doctor, and got into Elysian Gardens to do away with Septimus Pogue. But—I reminded myself—he had an alibi. So what? If this were a mystery novel, that would almost guarantee that he was guilty! Killers almost always have alibis.

Patch interrupted this reverie by asking, "So, what's it like to be McCabe's Watson?"

"I am *not*—"

"WHAT DID OSCAR wear for Halloween?" I asked Popcorn the next morning, All Saints' Day, when she brought me my decaf.

"His uniform hat."

"That must have fooled everybody." He usually covers his balding noggin with some other chapeau when not on duty, often a baseball cap but sometimes a straw Panama. "I hope that's not all he was wearing."

Before the morning banter could deteriorate any further, my phone rang.

"Good morning, Jefferson!" Mac boomed. "I regret to inform you that Clayton Belmont died last evening."

"What!"

"His son called Oscar this morning and demanded a meeting. I am sure you will realize that such an encounter is fraught with implications, given that the younger Belmont is not only a prominent member of the community but a candidate for city council. That is why Oscar called yours truly and requested my participation."

"And you're calling me because even Batman needs a Robin."

"Well put, old boy!"

Mac wasn't on speaker but was talking loud enough for Popcorn to hear. She mouthed "Do it!"

THE PARTY TOOK place in Oscar's conference room at police headquarters, which had been a vault back in the days when the building housed the Fifth National Bank of Erin, long ago absorbed into Gamble Bank. Roger Belmont wasn't thrilled to find Mac and me awaiting him when he arrived.

"What's he doing here?" he asked Oscar, nodding toward the big guy and ignoring me. "He practically accused my father of murdering Pogue!"

"Hardly that," Mac demurred.

"I invited him." The Chief leaned back and folded his hands over his corporation. "Professor McCabe is kind of like an unofficial consultant. You don't mind, do you?"

Belmont minded, but he didn't say so.

"Look, I'm here to demand an autopsy," he said.

"As the deceased's son, you have the right to do so," Oscar assured him. "But you need to talk to the coroner's office about that. It's not in my bailiwick."

"Dad was a perfectly healthy 86-year-old," Belmont went on, as if he needed to convince somebody. "I think he was poisoned, just like his old partner."

"By whom?" Mac asked.

"By whoever poisoned Pogue, which the Erin police don't seem to have made any progress in figuring out. I think maybe it's time for a review of this force's efficiency, most particularly its chief, which I will see to when I'm on council."

Mac and I had already heard Belmont sing that song at Malarkey's. Oscar looked like he wanted to say, "Over your dead body," but he didn't. Instead, he noted, "I'll tell you what I tell Adrian Pogue when he calls every day: We have no higher priority right now than solving his father's murder."

"Yes, you do—solving my father's murder."

"We don't know that your father was murdered, and in fact as of yet have no evidence that even points in that direction."

Mac butted in to ask Belmont, "How was your father's body found?"

"I called all that in. You can get it from listening to the 911 recording."

"Please humor me, Mr. Belmont."

Belmont took a deep *"why do I have to deal with this crap"* breath and said, "I'm the one who found him, and I'll never be able to forget it. I went over to help Dad hand out candy. There was no answer when I rang the doorbell, so I used my spare key to get in. I found him on the den floor." Belmont's voice broke then, and it took him a few moments to pick up the narrative again. "I didn't know at first that he was dead— I thought he was unconscious, maybe he'd fallen and hit his head. But he didn't have a pulse. That's when I called 911."

"It can scarcely matter to you that you have my condolences, but you do," Mac told him. "I am sure the circumstances of your father's unexpected departure only added to the pain. Septimus Pogue's family is also mourning his death, to which you alluded, as is the daughter-in-law of Ira Brown."

"You may remember that last one was a hit-and-run," Oscar interrupted to tell Belmont. "We never identified the driver."

"A suggestion has been made that Mr. Brown, who was suffering from depression, deliberately brought about his own death by stepping in front of the auto," Mac resumed. "There is another possibility, however. It could be that we are looking at a case of triple murder. Perhaps you should redouble your efforts to find the driver of that silver Honda, Oscar."

"Whatever it takes," Belmont said, "I expect you to find my father's killer before they die of old age."

Chapter Sixteen
Brothers

"ROGER BELMONT KILLED his father for his money," Popcorn asserted when I filled her in back at the office.

"How do you figure that?"

"It's obvious that he's trying to divert suspicion from himself by asking for an autopsy that's going to show his father was murdered. I mean, nobody would expect a killer to call attention to his crime."

"That sounds more like one of Mac's plots than those trashy Rosamund DeLacey romance novels you read—the old 'least likely suspect' plot. By that logic, Pogue should be guilty of his own murder because he asked for an autopsy."

"Technically, Boss, Mac asked for the autopsy on behalf of the family. Hey, better keep an eye on him!" She was enjoying this. "He did inherit from Pogue's death."

"But not Clay Belmont's."

"Which brings us back to Roger Belmont!"

And so on.

BUT THE MCCABE brain was going in a surprisingly different direction.

"What held those three partners together decades after their business had been terminated?" he asked me in an after-lunch phone call. "What made them 'blood brothers'?"

"I have no idea, but I deduce that you're going to tell me."

"Indeed I am, Jefferson! Frank Woodford related in his *Observer* column about Septimus that the fortunes of Pogue & Belmont had foundered due to the depredations of the funeral home's office manager, who subsequently disappeared, never to be seen again. Although it pains me to say this, what if one of the partners killed him in anger or retribution, and the guilty secret of his spilled blood was what made them 'blood brothers'? That would give someone, perhaps a relative, a motive for making away with the trio, would it not?"

"Where are you going with this?"

"Do you recall the name of the absconding employee?"

"Um, no."

"Nor did I, I must admit, until I went back to that "To Be Frank" column. He was Stephen Collier, and the obituary notice which I found in the *Observer* lists Wesley Collier—of the Collier insurance agency—as his brother. Suggestive, is it not?"

"Only to a highly suggestible person."

"Come, come, old boy! Stephen Collier's brother had a business relationship with all three partners in that funeral home and they are now all dead."

"We don't even know that Stephen Collier was killed, or that the partners killed him, but let's say they did. How do you get from there to the revenge motive? If Wes Collier, or anybody, was getting even for a murder that you speculate happened in—when was it? 1989—why wait this long?"

"Perhaps Mr. Collier only recently realized his brother is dead and that they are responsible."

"SO FAR AS I know, my brother is still alive," Wes Collier told us. He looked miserable behind his dark glasses, as if he'd rather be at Bobbie McGee's hoisting a few than behind his desk at the Collier Agency facing Mac and me. But then, who wouldn't?

"What makes you think so?" Mac asked.

"He sent my mother a postcard from Costa Rica that said he was sorry about everything and not worry about him. I can't quote it exactly. I stopped looking at it years ago, but Mom didn't. She kept it on her dresser until the day she died two years ago—bad heart, the doctor said, but I always thought it was a heart broken by Steve, really. She talked about him like he might come back any day."

Mac opened his mouth to ask a question, but Collier went on as if the flood gates of memory had been jarred open.

"Steve was the much older brother I looked up to— sixteen years older than me, with three sisters in between our births. I was eighteen when he disappeared and the whole thing about him stealing money from Pogue & Belmont came out. I'm sure you remember it."

That was a couple of years before I followed Kate to Erin, but it didn't seem worth interrupting Collier to say so. He talked on without waiting for Mac or me to comment.

"Dad's business here at the Collier Agency took a hit for a while. People must have been thinking the apple didn't fall far from the tree. I mean, Steve ripped off his employer and people probably thought he learned it somewhere. Nobody said that, but it was in the air. Dad never mentions his name. He probably threw away the postcard after Mom died. He's still alive, you know—Dad is. Ninety-two years old and living at Elysian Gardens. There's irony for you."

I'm not sure that's irony. Coincidence, maybe.

"You told us the last time we talked with you that Ira Brown was a lodge brother of your father's and that's probably why he got the partners' insurance, but you didn't mention your brother's connection to the funeral home," I said.

"It's not my favorite topic of conversation." He sat forward. "Do you have children, Mr. Cody?"

"I certainly do. Three of the little cherubs."

"Would they be financially secure if something happened to you?"

"Is that a threat?"

"I believe it is what is known as a sales pitch, Jefferson," Mac said.

"I'm well insured through the university," I assured Collier.

Mac changed the topic: "Are you familiar with that post card that was so cherished by your mother?"

"You could say that," Collier replied. "Mom showed it to me often enough."

"Was the message on it printed rather than in cursive?"

If I could have seen Collier's eyes, I bet I would have seen them widen. "How the hell did you know that?"

"Because cursive handwriting is distinctive to the individual who wrote it. And I sincerely doubt your brother wrote that postcard, Mr. Collier. Nor do I believe he is alive."

"Holy shit!"

As soon as we were out the door of Collier's office and onto Spring Street, I said to Mac, "That interview wasn't what you expected, was it?"

He sighed. "No."

"Elucidate." I love throwing a big word at him now and again.

"I consider the printed postcard to be strong circumstantial evidence that Stephen Collier is dead, as I had surmised. The devil of it is, if Wesley Collier avenged his death by killing his former employers, he would want us to believe that his brother was still alive. Therefore, he would have told us the postcard was in his brother's handwriting so as to calm my suspicions that his brother didn't write it."

"Maybe he's just not that shrewd."

"Perhaps not, but I believe he would be sufficiently paranoid. 'The guilty flee,' etc."

"So, Stephen Collier was probably murdered thirty-four years ago by somebody who didn't want his parents—or anybody, I guess—to know that he was dead. But who? We have no evidence, and I don't see a way to get any after all this time. And how does that theorized murder fit in with the killing of Pogue and the rest?"

"Hell and damnation, Jefferson, I wish I knew the answer to the latter! As to the former, I fear that I know all too well."

Chapter Seventeen
Death and Love

THE NEXT DAY, Thursday, found me in a hardhat at the site of the rising Ezra Bainbridge Building with Mac and a reporter for Cincinnati's TV4.

Jason Sanchez was a short, energetic recent graduate of the E.W. Scripps School of Journalism at Ohio University, Lynda's alma mater, who was shouldering his own camera as his ilk in medium-sized television markets do these days for less-than-major assignments. He wanted to talk with someone about the SBU benefactor for whom the building was named, and I offered him Mac as a good friend of the late Ezra.

"So, I hear this guy Bainbridge's entire family was wiped out," he said while adjusting the camera. His breath was visible in the cold November air like cigar smoke.

"That's a bit of an exaggeration," I said. *His wife is still alive.*

My job at this point was to move Sanchez off that unpleasant subject without seeming too directional.

"There's no doubt the Bainbridge name is associated with a tragedy which is still in our minds two years later," I went on. "But Professor McCabe can talk to you about Ezra's love of the university which he served so long and so well as a member of the board of trustees, and his generous bequest."

"Let's do it!" Sanchez said.

Mac held forth at length, the only way he knows how to hold forth, and I have to admit that he was good. The parts that were used that night on the news included:

"Ezra Bainbridge was a man of significant inherited wealth, which he believed to be his in trust and not to be used for his personal gratification only. Hence his multimillion-dollar gift to St. Benignus University upon his passing. Ezra's devotion to the works of William Shakespeare makes it particularly appropriate that his name will grace this exciting new structure in the Rev. Joseph F. Pirelli School of Arts and Humanities."

When Mac came up for air, Sanchez said, "But isn't it true that his entire family . . ."

Well, I tried.

While the reporter started folding up his camera, I noticed a familiar-looking woman in her mid-fifties crush a cigarette beneath her gym shoe, step off the sidewalk, and amble toward us. Graying hair spilled over her down coat, and she folded her arms against her chest for warmth.

"Professor McCabe?" she called as she walked.

"At your service," he said.

Sanchez muttered his thanks and hustled off to the next assignment.

"I'm Trudi Belmont, Roger's wife. I'm sort of a friend of Kate's."

Looney Ladies Gallery, the late-lamented women's art cooperative! That's where I'd seen her before—during one of my sister's exhibits of her watercolors. She'd been one of the other artists, although I hadn't paid attention to her name at the time and certainly never connected her to the scooter-averse Roger Belmont.

"A pleasure," Mac informed her.

"I know my husband's been a burr up your ass about you talking to Clay in connection with the Pogue murder, Professor McCabe," she went on.

"Those are not the words I would have chosen, Mrs. Belmont." *Not enough syllables.*

"I love my husband, but he can be a challenge when he gets an idea in his head." *Take banning electric scooters, for instance.* It occurred to me that Trudi Belmont and Cindy LeVan should start a support group for each other. "You have to understand that his mother left for another man when Roger was a kid, and Clay pretty much raised him by himself. There was no other child, so it was just the two of them. Roger's whole life has been trying to make his dad proud of his success. And now Clay's gone and it's hard for Roger to believe that he was mortal like everybody else."

"All of that is understandable, and I take no offense at your husband's aggressive pursuit of the truth. Nor, I am confident, does Chief Hummel." *He's used to being hassled by oddballs with recently dead fathers.*

"It sounds like you don't think your father-in-law was murdered," I said.

"The autopsy presumably will settle that, but it doesn't seem likely, does it? Not unless there's some connection to the murder of his old partner, Septimus Pogue."

And to the death of Ira Brown, I thought.

"Anyway," Trudi Belmont concluded, "I just wanted to apologize on Roger's behalf and ask for your understanding. Say hi to Kate for me. I'll give her a call sometime."

I WAS SURPRISED to see a small story without a byline at the bottom of the local page in Friday's *Observer*: **POLICE SEEK HIT-AND-RUN DRIVER**.

> Erin Police are still looking for the driver of a late model Honda Civic, silver in color, which struck and killed Ira Brown, 74, on the afternoon of Oct. 2 on Front Street, near the corner of High Street. Brown was mortally injured and died several days later.
>
> Anyone who may have seen the accident and can provide any information is asked to call Assistant Chief L. Jack Gibbons at . . .

"Oscar's taking the Ira Brown angle seriously, and rightly so," I told Lynda over breakfast. "Three former partners dead within weeks can't be a coincidence."

She looked up from her horoscope. "Sure it can. Besides, they were partners in the last century. That's not the closest connection in the world. Oh, I forgot to tell you. I have Lily Inouye lined up to babysit tonight."

We'd decided to cough up the young lady's sky-high hourly fee to have a romantic night out at Ricoletti's Ristorante, Erin's most elegant eatery. Offering a hilltop view of the Ohio River, it had originally been a riverboat captain's house and a stop on the Underground Railroad. Both of those features were true of Mac's house as well, but Ricoletti's is, of course, much bigger, with a number of dining rooms. And cocktail hour that night found us in one of them, with lovely Lynda dressed to the nines in a curve-hugging little black DYNK number and the cameo necklace I bought her in a Vatican gift shop on our honeymoon.

"It's so nice to have adult conversation uninterrupted by three rambunctious kids," Lynda said as she sipped her Manhattan. The intoxicating scent of her Cleopatra VII perfume, pricey but worth it, wafted across the table.

"You're missing them, aren't you?"

"Absolutely. Hey, isn't that Lexi Pogue just coming in?" She nodded discreetly toward the wedding-planning magician. "I saw her picture with Johanna's *Observer* story."

You might be thinking the bald head was a give-away, but Lexi was wearing a wool felt cloche hat, red, that played nicely off her tan coat. She was accompanied by a man about half a foot shorter, roughly her age, decked out in blue-framed glasses, jeans, and a white shirt with French cuffs beneath a corduroy jacket. His hair was shaggy and darkish. This was clearly the slow-to-commit boyfriend to whom she had alluded. The couple sat down, and Lynda and I resumed our adult conversation.

Half-through my salmon, I heard a shriek from Lexi's end of the room and saw a waiter come over to her table with a bottle of Asti Spumante as she held out her hand to admire a sparkling diamond ring.

"Remind you of anything?" Lynda asked, her voice sounding particularly husky as it does when she's in a certain mood.

"The night we celebrated our engagement here," I said, passing the test. "I'll never forget it. Enzo Ricoletti himself provided the bubbly on the house. It was a great night."

"We've had many great nights, *tesoro mio*." She waggled her eyebrows suggestively.

Suddenly I wanted to get home, and not to play with the kids. But we finished dinner, ate tiramisu for dessert, and lingered a bit over decaf cappuccino to savor the mood and the memories. As we were on our way out, Lexi Pogue waved a hand and hailed, "Jeff!"

We detoured.

"It doesn't take a Sebastian McCabe to deduce that you two are celebrating," Lynda said.

I introduced her and Lexi announced, "This is my fiancé as of a few minutes ago, Jack."

He stood, though not very tall, to shake our hands firmly while wearing a grin that seemed natural enough.

"Don't make him disappear," I advised Lexi.

"Our engagement hashtag is #LoveIsMagic," was her response. She didn't just make that up on the spot, I was sure, but Lynda proclaimed it "so cute" and added, "I hope you two will be as happily married as we are."

A lovely evening to be sure—and yet, something nagged at me about it. Something that I'd seen or heard at Ricoletti's had something to do with Septimus Pogue's murder, but I had no idea what it was. That bothered me the rest of the weekend, simmering at a low level in the back of my mind.

"MAYBE YOU SHOULD have Mac hypnotize you, like he did Justin Bird in that *1895* murder case and you in that Fourth of July business," Popcorn suggested on Monday morning during our coffee ritual. "Whatever you're trying to think of is there in your subconscious. You just have to pry it out."

"Say, that's not a half-bad idea! You've had a lot worse."

"Thanks, Boss. I think."

I picked up the phone to call Mac. But before I could get to his name on my call list, he called me. (The days when everybody had ringtones and his was "You're So Vain" seem so long ago.)

"Cody's Criminous Capers," I answered. Before I could go any further down that line, Mac interrupted with:

"Alas, Jefferson, this is no time for attempted levity. The killer of Ira Brown has just confessed to me here in my office, and his identity has implications for you as communications director."

I MADE IT to Herbert Hall in record time, arriving to find a young man with "student" written all over him slumped in the chair I usually occupy on my visits to Mac's firetrap. He was bulky, a football-player type, and he looked like he hadn't slept in days.

"This is Mark Williams, a senior and one of the less distinguished students in my Twentieth Century Poetry class," Mac said. "He ran over Mr. Brown. If he came to me this morning to confess in the belief that I can help him avoid the full consequences of his actions because of my well-known connection with Chief Hummel, he is much mistaken."

"It's not like I meant to do it!" Williams cried. "Like I told you, he ran in front of me. I couldn't stop."

My stomach lurched at the unbidden mental image of that scene. "You could have stopped afterwards," I snapped. "You could have made sure the old man got medical help."

"I panicked, dude. I wasn't thinking. Then, when I saw on social media that he died and the cops were looking for me, I didn't have the balls to turn myself in."

"Your lack of testicular fortitude is indeed unfortunate, Mr. Williams," Mac said in a scathing tone. "It caused an unnecessary measure of additional suffering for the deceased's family."

"Yeah, I know."

"What caused you to man up?" I wondered.

"I live at home. My mother read me a story in the paper on Friday that said they were still looking for me. I figured it was just a matter of time. Plus, you know, I feel bad about it. I think about it all the time." For what it's worth (not much) that sounded true. "What happens now?"

"The Sacrament of Reconciliation would be a good move, though the state of your soul is none of my business," Mac said. "I brought in Mr. Cody because the university administration would not want to be blind-sided by the fallout of your belated confession. That is the least of your concerns, however.

"Mr. Cody and I will accompany you to the police station. You may wish to call an attorney on the way. Perhaps he or she can reach a plea bargain based on the fact that you did come forward, however belatedly. Also, Chief Hummel told us that one of the witnesses reported that Mr. Brown virtually threw himself at your car, supporting your account."

"They did?"

A ray of hope! Which Mac was quick to dash, not being in a coddling mood.

"You still ran over a man and left the scene," he said. "Your future is bleak. However, at least you have a future, which is not the case for the late Mr. Brown."

The rest of my day was pretty much taken up with the spillover from Williams's confession. We got the miscreant to Oscar, where he was met by a young lawyer from SladeLaw—formerly the Slade Law Firm—named Sally Fair. I knew Sally slightly as a member of Triple M's science fiction reading club, the Captain Nemo Society. It turned out that Williams's mother was a member of the old-money Harridan family, so that a court-appointed lawyer would not be necessary. I conferred with my boss, Saylor-Mackie, who bucked it up to G.K., who called Sarah Fink-Brown (with me in his office) to express sympathy and to subtly let her know that although an SBU student killed her father it was SBU employees who helped bring him to justice. Johanna's subsequent story in the *Observer* made the bottom of page one.

By the end of the day, I was looking forward to cocktail hour at Chez Cody. But one more hit was coming. Just before I left the office, Oscar sent a group text to Mac and me:

> *Arly shared Clay Belmont autopsy results. No poison. Died of aortic aneurism.*

And with that, the whole somebody-killed-all-three-former-partners scenario was as dead as Jacob Marley, but wouldn't be showing up as a ghost. We were back to Square One, or possibly Square Zero.

Chapter Eighteen

Hiding in Plain Sight?

I VOTED EARLY on Tuesday, but not for Zoraida Quant and not—despite my earlier temptation—for Roger Belmont. Quant might hex city council, and Belmont might vex Oscar.

"I'm not worried about that stuffed shirt," Oscar assured us about the latter over sandwiches in his conference room at lunchtime. The long table was laden with take-out, napkins, and drinks. "He looks pretty foolish going ballistic on me about his father's murder that wasn't a murder."

"Only to us," I said. "The older Belmont may have been 86, but he looked in the pink. I can see why his son was suspicious, what with his former partners checking out so recently."

But it was time to bring this confab to the real business at hand, and I was just the guy to do it. "Anyway, minus that distraction, we're back to what we started with: The murder of—sorry, Mac—one elderly gent in a nursing home who was on his way out anyway. The angel of death could have been Clay Belmont—"

"I'd rather it was Roger," Oscar quipped.

"—since we now know that he himself wasn't murdered by the nursing home killer."

"There is no indication that the elder Belmont was at Elysian Gardens that day," Mac observed. "Of course, that is no stumbling block. We have already posited that the killer could have been in some sort of disguise—although I must say the disguise options for a man of the elder Mr. Belmont's age are somewhat limited. There is also the matter of motive. Surely, the pull of avarice must diminish as one gets older and has less time to enjoy one's wealth."

"Are you kidding?" Oscar huffed. "Have you ever seen a billionaire shy away from adding to his pile? Or give it all away while he was still alive?"

If I were fully engaged in this conversation, I could have joined in with some observations about foundations or astute comments about estate planning, but I was stuck on my own use of the term "nursing home killer." That reminded me of Donald Harvey and the Elysian Gardens' John Rentz. And all of a sudden, I knew what had been bothering the Cody brain since that night at Ricoletti's.

"Wait!" I almost shouted. "What if Sable Pogue was right about the nursing home attendant killing her father?"

"Rentz wasn't working the day of the murder," Oscar said. "We checked him out."

"Right. He was supposedly sick, and definitely a terrible employee soon to get the boot. But even a terrible employee with a desire to play God would know his way around well enough to keep from being spotted on his way to injecting fentanyl into a patient's drip line."

"And Septimus just happened to be the unfortunate victim of his attentions, I suppose," Mac rumbled.

This is where it gets sweet, I thought.

"Not at all. Ever since I met Lexi's fiancé on Friday night something's been bothering me. And today when I heard me say 'nursing home,' it clicked. The lucky man is named Jack, and Jack is a nickname for John—as in John Rentz." Mac and Oscar's faces told me that they were stunned by my brilliance. Or at least stunned. Even Holly Burdette, Oscar's executive assistant, paused in the act of walking past the conference room door to hear me expound.

"And his motive?" Mac asked.

"That's obvious. In talking to us early on, Lexi referred to her 'slow to commit' boyfriend. But after she inherited from her grandfather, voilà, he's committed and now they're going to have an undoubtedly well-planned wedding so that Jack benefits from Pogue's death!"

"Ohio is not a community property state, Jefferson."

"Still."

"Also, Lexi's inheritance is limited to Septimus's cat, his Checker cab, and the magic collection."

"And as we saw close up, collectors are tripping over themselves to buy Harry Keller's magic wand and whatnot. That stuff is probably worth hundreds of thousands of bucks. Which is a good segue to the other possibility: Maybe Lexi, not Jack, is the brains behind the murder."

I hated to say it, but there it was.

Both of the McCabe eyebrows shot up.

"This is fascinating," Holly opined from the hallway with a can of maximum caffeine in her hand.

Oscar, who had been watching Mac and me bandy words like ping-pong balls, stepped in with:

"Why would the instigator of the murder ask Mac to poke into the case?"

I chuckled. "Because her head hasn't been under a rock for the last decade. She knew that he would get involved come hell or high water, so she figured the best thing to do was to get close to him by asking for his help. It's the old 'client is the killer ploy,' which Popcorn thought was at work in the Belmont murder, which wasn't really a murder.

"So," I summarized, "there you have two possible scenarios for Lexi's fiancé killing Septimus Pogue—on his own initiative or upon request from his lady love."

"Both of which hinge on him being John Rentz," Mac noted.

"Which he isn't," Holly tossed in from the hallway. "Like I said, all this brainwork has been fascinating, but Lexi's boyfriend is Jack Tanner, who works for a small design firm in northern Kentucky."

"How do you know all that?" Oscar asked, a note of almost fatherly pride in his voice.

"Social media, of course. Their engagement hashtag is #LoveIsMagic. How cool is that?"

She and her energy drink departed.

I was too stunned to comment.

"Incidentally, Jefferson," Mac said, "if Alexandra were behind Septimus's murder, she would have certainly destroyed the letter asking to have a postmortem performed and no one would have suspected that his death was anything other than natural causes."

"Oh."

"The problem with you guys," Oscar lectured, "is that you make things too complicated."

"Actually, it usually is complicated," I pointed out. "That's why you need McCabe & Cody to solve it."

"Oh, is that why? Then solve it!"

Mac thumped his hand on the table, causing his mostly empty cup of coffee to vibrate. "By thunder, I think you are on to something, Oscar."

"Like what?" I wondered.

"The solution to this case is a simple one."

"And that is what?" Oscar asked before I could. But just then his cell rang. "Hell's bells," was his reaction when he saw who was calling. That was followed by, "Hello, Mayor" as he answered. To my surprise, he then activated the speaker function so we could listen in. Or maybe provide moral support.

"Hello, Chief," came the sonorous voice of Mayor Fred Sutterlee, honed by years in the pulpit as senior pastor of the Apostolic Holiness Church of the Holy Spirit, and further polished by singing with Rabbi Goldman and Father O'Boyle in the Joyful Noise tenor trio. "I'm just calling with a word of encouragement. The Septimus Pogue murder is receiving more than the usual amount of attention outside of our fair city, but I have complete confidence that you can solve it and bring justice and righteousness."

Oscar glowed. "Thank you, Mayor. I really appreciate that."

"I'm not on the ballot this year, but I hope you voted or will."

"I did."

Not for Roger Belmont, I bet. And not for Zoraida Quant, I hope.

"Good. Call me if I can be of any help. Good-bye, Chief. And good-bye, Professor McCabe." He disconnected.

Oscar stared at his phone. "How did he know—never mind. What were you saying about a simple solution to this case, Mac?"

"It would be premature for me to expound at this point."

ON THE WAY back to campus, Mac could have given the Sphynx lessons in taciturnity. All my attempts to wheedle out of him what he was thinking were useless. But not long after I'd returned to my office and settled in to writing a speech for G.K., he called me.

"I had a notion, Jefferson, which led to a question for Dr. Abington—and the answer was what I suspected."

When he told me what that was, I almost fell off my chair.

"In all fairness we must concede that Oscar was right to chide us for overthinking," he said. "We neglected Occam's Razor that the simplest solution is usually the right one. I console myself that the simple, correct solution in front of us the whole time was concealed by a misdirection worthy of the Great Blackstone himself. After a few preparations, we can ring down the curtain on this affair in an appropriately dramatic way tomorrow night. And I believe the long-unused stage of Magic Unlimited would be the perfect venue."

Chapter Nineteen
On Stage

ZORAIDA QUANT FINISHED 22nd in a field of 22 vying for nine seats on city council. Roger Belmont sneaked in at number nine, to the terror of electric scooter riders all over town. But local politics wasn't top of mind for me as I awaited Mac's big reveal, scheduled for 7 P.M. the day after the election.

"You know what he has up his sleeve, don't you?" Popcorn said during our morning coffeeklatch.

"Well, yes. So does Oscar. Did he tell you?"

She scowled. "No."

"Then I won't either. My lips are sealed." *Pillow talk at the Cody residence last night was an exception.* "How's Riley doing with engagement on our Facebook page?"

I didn't hear her answer. The word 'engagement' made me think of Lexi Pogue. My mind wandered off in her direction and I found it hard to concentrate on work the rest of the day.

She and the fiancé, Jack-not-John, were waiting to let us in when we showed up outside the former Magic Unlimited shortly before 6:30 that evening. Quant gave us the evil eye from across the street, but she wasn't invited to the soiree. Jack Tanner didn't say much, but Lexi did.

"What's going on?" she demanded of Mac. "You said on the phone you know who killed Granddad. Is this where you do that whole *Death in Paradise* 'round up the suspects' thing?"

Yes, but he won't admit it.

"I prefer to think of it as an opportunity for all involved in this sad affair to learn the results of my investigation at the same time," Mac replied.

Translation: "Yes, but I won't admit it."

"Including Aunt Sable and Dad?"

"Of course."

Those two were among the first to arrive, Sable looking curious, and her brother looking put out. They even beat Oscar, Lt. Col. L. Jack Gibbons, and Officers Bertsch and Mentzel. Then came Wes Collier, Councilman-elect Belmont with wife Trudi, Sarah Fink-Brown, Dr. Abington, Lafcadio Figg, and Lexi's stepmother, Cindy LeVan. By 7 P.M. the small shop was crowded with citizens wearing "why the hell am I here" expressions on their faces. Except for Johanna Rawls—she knew why she was there: to watch Sebastian McCabe pull the proverbial rabbit out of the proverbial hat. She'd promised Mac to fade into the wall and not say anything until the denouement.

Mac, aided by his walking stick with the hound's head, mounted the small stage to say:

"Thank you all for coming. What will unfold this evening will be painful to some, perhaps gratifying to others, and enlightening to all."

"Get on with it," Adrian Pogue snapped.

"All right then," Mac said. "Here is the painful truth—painful to me as much as to anyone here—that needs to be acknowledged first: The original sin in this case was the death of Stephen Collier, office manager of the former Pogue & Belmont, at the hands of his employers. My heart rejects the notion, but my head tells me the facts are there."

In plainspeak, Mac had just called the late Ira Brown, Septimus Pogue, and Clayton Belmont murderers in front of their families. The collective gasp in response, which had to be satisfying to the McCabe ego, was followed by overlapping exclamations of incredulity. I think Lexi said something like "batshit crazy," while her aunt preferred "off your gourd." I don't know what, if anything, Adrian said, but Roger Belmont opted for "outrageous," and Sarah Fink-Brown found Mac's characterization of her father-in-law to be "unbelievable."

Oscar looked worried that Mac had finally stepped into something unpleasant, while L. Jack Gibbons—a man who never uses two words when one will do—remained impassive as usual. Gibbons is, after all, a man who engages in axe throwing on dates with my friend Aurelia Banfield, assistant chief of the St. Benignus University Police.

"I thought something like that was coming," Wes Collier said when the hubbub settled a bit. "Why else invite me to this shindig? But I've been thinking about it, McCabe. That whole business you handed me of deciding if Steve's still alive because he printed a postcard instead of writing it is pretty thin stuff."

"I have proof of his demise, Mr. Collier. However, that need not detain us at this moment. For now, it is enough to say that I have stated a fact. Your brother is not alive, I am sorry to tell you. However, it may give you and your father some satisfaction to know that neither was he a thief."

"What! Dad will shit a brick," I heard Collier mutter. Then, louder, he asked: "Why did they kill him?"

"All in good time, Mr. Collier. You have waited this long; I ask you to wait just a little longer. First, I wish to explain the more recent homicide.

"Solving the murder of Septimus Pogue was really just a matter of clearing away the brush to see the essential situation. Chief Hummel made me see that by suggesting that I was overcomplicating matters in my search for a solution." He nodded toward Oscar, who tried without success to avoid looking pleased. "What happened as a result of that original sin ultimately led to the more recent murder. To wit: The three men bound together by their co-responsibility for the death of Stephen Collier agreed to maintain their life insurance on each other after they sold what was left of their doomed business. Septimus and Mr. Belmont both benefited from the death of Ira Brown because they were still alive when he died. Then Septimus was murdered not long thereafter. Mr. Belmont was named in Septimus's policy, of course, but was also the contingent beneficiary of the money that would have gone to Mr. Brown had he been alive."

"Now you're saying flat-out that my father killed Pogue?" Roger Belmont's face was flushed against his brown hair and the eyes behind his glasses were on fire. "How dare you!"

"Not your father, Mr. Belmont," Mac corrected. "You. When all the smoke has cleared—the misdirection caused by your theft of the trunk and then by pretending to believe your father was murdered—the irreducible fact is that you, as your father's only child, presumably inherit all the money your father gained from those insurance policies of his former partners. And you are sorely in need of it. I am fairly confident that your father had no suspicion of your guilt, even though he must have told you in all innocence about the insurance tontine in your double capacity as his financial advisor and heir."

Belmont gave a hollow chuckle, obviously forced, and glanced at his wife, who looked like she'd been sucker-punched by a Boy Scout. "Speaking of smoke, McCabe, you're blowing it. Everybody knows that I'm a highly successful financial advisor."

At this retort the mutton-chopped Figg appeared to be calculating the cost of Belmont's expensive-looking knit pullover, which I later found out cost well north of $500 retail. But Mac continued with:

"As the operator of the local J&J Littlejohn office, you naturally feel required to project an aura of pecuniary success to your clients. However, I feel certain that an exploration of your own investments would find that you were one of the many casualties of what has been called 'crypto winter,' the collapse last year of crypto currency."

"He's the one who got me into FTX!" Sable Pogue exploded. "That was a disaster."

Belmont winced, opened his mouth, then shut it again.

Mac nodded. "In our conversation with you at your niece's house, Ms. Pogue, you told us you 'took a flyer' in crypto on your financial advisor's advice and that he was 'big into it.' Later, Mr. Belmont, you mentioned that Ms. Pogue was one of your clients. Ergo, it is not an unreasonable assumption your own losses on cryptocurrency must have been significant.

"You knew, however, that when your father died you would receive an inheritance that would allow you to recoup those losses and perhaps more. And upon Ira Brown's sad demise, that potential inheritance grew as a result of the insurance policy in your father's name. You must have learned about the tontine from your father then, if not before. Over lunch on Saturday at Malarkey's Pub you pretended ignorance of it, and yet when told of the insurance policies from which your father benefited you did not ask the amount. It beggars the imagination that even an outwardly successful wealth advisor would not be curious.

"Undoubtedly, you knew the amount. And you also knew that you would inherit even more upon your father's death if Septimus Pogue died before him so that he could also benefit from the policy Septimus took out in his name. You ultimately profited from the deaths of all three 'blood brothers.'"

"But Clay Belmont wasn't murdered," objected Dr. Abington. "He died of an inoperable aortic aneurism that he knew he had. It turned up in a routine scan. Dr. Sharfman was his cardiologist. He had been a ticking time bomb for some time even though he looked fine."

Mac nodded. "And as you yourself told me when I asked you, Doctor, Roger Belmont knew that. You discussed the diagnosis with his father in his presence as part of a routine visit. Roger's pretense not to know about it, even questioning whether his father was murdered, was misdirection to draw attention away from his clear motive for murder—that motive being the necessity that Septimus Pogue die before his father."

As I write this, it strikes me that Popcorn was close to being right when she said that Roger's cage-rattling about his father's death—insisting on an autopsy—was a smokescreen. But it wasn't, as she thought, guilt for Clay's murder that he was trying to obscure; it was his knowledge that the old man was terminal.

"However great your filial piety, learning that your father was not long for this fallen world must have initially given you the comfort of knowing that your secret financial woes would soon be relieved," Mac told Belmont. "Upon further reflection, however, you must have realized the implications of the third part to that pact: If Clayton Belmont died before Septimus Pogue, then Septimus—and shortly thereafter, his heirs—would receive that insurance payout from the policy Clayton took out on his behalf. How unfair that must have seemed to you! But it need not be so. If only Septimus Pogue died first, your father would get the payout from Septimus's insurance on him instead—plus a second payout as the contingent beneficiary of the policy made out in the late Ira Brown's name—and thereafter you would benefit from both. Your father knew that Septimus was near death at Elysian Gardens, and you must have known it from him, but it was far from guaranteed that he would die first, as indeed he may not have if not for his murder."

"You bastard!" Lexi spat at Roger Belmont. Adrian Pogue put his arm around his daughter, and she didn't pull away. Cindy LeVan, the ex-stepmother, stepped closer as Lexi added: "What do you have to say for yourself?"

"I say this is a fantasy dreamed up by a fiction writer." Belmont's tone was defiant. But if I read the room right, his wife was the only one buying that line. She grabbed his hand. Belmont addressed Oscar: "Stop this charade, Chief! I'm a city councilman-elect."

"You're also a suspect, and I'd say a pretty good one," the Chief retorted.

"You're wrong!" Trudi Belmont protested. "My husband is a good man."

Mac stayed admirably calm in his reply, considering that we were talking about the murder of his mentor. "Whatever your husband's virtues—and good judgement is certainly not one of them—he must have convinced himself he had two million good reasons for speeding a dying man on his way to glory."

The devil is a busy dude.

"How did he do it?" Sable Pogue asked.

"Would you care to answer?" Mac asked Belmont.

"I'd rather hear your fairy tale, McCabe."

Mac nodded. "All right, then. I shall have to speculate. You clearly have difficulty walking as a result of the electric scooter accident that put you in the hospital, Mr. Belmont. The severe pain experienced probably led to a prescription for fentanyl patches. Care to comment, Dr. Abington?"

He shook his head. "Roger's not my patient, and I couldn't comment if he was. But it sounds plausible. And if he had access to fentanyl—"

"Exactly," Mac said. "Internet research shows that it is relatively easy to suck the drug out of a fentanyl patch with a syringe."

"Then what?" Sarah Fink-Brown asked. "How did he walk into Elysian Gardens and inject the fentanyl into the line?" I put the query down to the curiosity of someone who worked in a medical facility.

"Most likely he dressed as some sort of service worker, such as housekeeping or food service. At any rate, after the deed was done there was one loose end that had to be cut off. Septimus must have told his erstwhile partners that he maintained a different kind of insurance policy on his life. He wrote a statement detailing their joint crime that was left to me as part of my legacy, to be opened in the event of his murder. Mr. Belmont, presumably informed by his father about the document, correctly surmised that it was in the magician's trunk left to me in Septimus's will, which he learned about from reading Frank Woodford's column in the *Observer*. He stole the trunk by breaking into Magic Unlimited—"

"How did he know it was there?" Tall Rawls burst out, no longer a silent observer.

Belmont assumed a "yeah—what about that?" look on his face.

"Where better to look for a magician's trunk than in a magic store?" Mac replied. "He subsequently disposed of it by leaving it to be found backstage at the Lyceum—minus a certain fireproof box."

"Why there, of all places?" Lafcadio Figg wanted to know.

"Ah, that takes us firmly back into the realm of speculation. I suspect that his intention was to frame you for the theft of the trunk, Lafcadio, having observed at the reception after Septimus's memorial both your interest in vintage baseball cards and the somewhat—shall we say—contentious interplay between the two of us."

Instead of commenting on that, Belmont said: "You have absolutely no evidence for this pipe dream, McCabe, and I'm bitterly disappointed that our police chief stands silent while you defame a member of city council."

That's "member-elect!"

Mac was in his element now, and it showed in the glow of his broad and bearded phiz.

"Au contraire, Mr. Belmont!" he rumbled. "I am confident that the video cameras outside of Elysian Gardens will show you arriving on the day of the murder, wearing a service uniform of some sort and slight disguise not beyond penetration by those looking for it."

"Officer Lehman is working on that now," Gibbons reported.

"Thank you, Col. Gibbons! Excellent! And the box?"

"I have it right here."

Gibbons held up what I knew to be a small fireproof box for storing important papers. I also knew that Mac had already not only seen the box but opened it. What followed was just theater, appropriately carried out on stage.

"That's mine!" Belmont all but shouted. "How did you get it?"

"Search warrant," Gibbons said. "Your son let us in this afternoon."

Probably a good reason to invite adult children to move out.

"It is not, however, yours," Mac told Belmont. "It belonged to Septimus Pogue, who willed it to me as part of the contents of the magician's trunk that you stole. That will be proven by the contents."

Is that sweat on your forehead, Roger?

"Are you going to break it open, adding destruction of private property to the charges when I file suit?"

"That will not be necessary. The combination lock to open the box requires four numbers. Septimus said in his letter to me, 'Sherlockian that you are, I'm sure you can figure out the numbers.' There is a particular year in the late Victorian era that has symbolic significance for us devotees of

Sherlock Holmes, who like to say—in the words of Vincent Starrett's immortal sonnet—'it is always 1895.'" As he said the last word, Mac brought up those numbers on the combination lock. It clicked softly.

He opened the box and brought out two items. First, a wallet. Mac opened that, too, and held it up, showing a driver's license with a photo.

"That's my brother!" Wes Collier exclaimed. "That's Steve."

Then Mac pulled out a business-size envelope. "And this is Septimus Pogue's account of Stephen Collier's killing and the other crime with which the three partners were involved. That has only a tangential connection to the business at hand in that it explains the reason for the insurance tontine. However, your possession of it, Mr. Belmont, proves that you stole the magician's trunk, the lesser of your two crimes."

Adrenaline rush can enable the human body to do amazing things. Despite his bum leg, Belmont bolted. And first after him—even ahead of Gibbons, Bertsch, and Mentzel—was the tall figure of Lexi Pogue. I was behind them, not close, but I kept them in sight for the entertainment value. Downtown Erin after-hours isn't exactly crowded, so I got a good view of Belmont as he pushed a young man, probably an SBU student, off an electric scooter and took command of the vehicle.

And promptly ran it into a telephone pole on Broadway.

By this time Gibbons had got ahead of Lexi, and he was halfway through giving Belmont the Miranda warning by the time she caught up.

Back at the Magic Unlimited shop, I later learned, Mac was entertaining his guests by reading aloud what was in the envelope that was in the box that was in the magician's trunk.

Chapter Twenty
A Dead Man Tells a Tale

March 16, 1996

MY FORMER PARTNERS and I were all in this together, mutually guilty, so I went along with Clay Belmont's idea of maintaining the life insurance on each other after we broke up the business. It's a way of acknowledging our responsibility to each other. We're all in this sordid business, and always will be even though we had to go our separate ways, businesswise. But a lot of money is involved, and murder is a slippery slope. If one of them does away with me for the insurance, I want to be sure that he pays for it. That's why I'm writing this.

Where to start? I suppose I should begin by saying in my defense that I never wanted to be in the funeral home business to begin with. My mother guilt-tripped me into it after my father's death. It was just Pogue Funeral Services until I brought in Clay Belmont fresh out of mortuary school. We had a good run for almost 30 years.

Then Hawes & Holder started eating our lunch. Holder is a master at preparing the deceased for viewings, I have to admit that. Month after month Stephen Collier, our office manager, would report numbers in the red. It was Clay's idea to fight back by teaming up with Ira Brown and his crematorium. That helped, but we were barely making it until Clay came up with the idea of getting into what's called the "red market"—selling body parts to medical training laboratories instead of cremating them. There wouldn't be a name for it if that didn't happen a lot. Selling body parts is legal with permission of the relatives, or upon the instructions of the deceased, but not the way we did it. We gave the bereaved cremains that were only parts of their beloved.

We made a good deal of money at it for a while, but there was bad karma attached. Eventually Collier caught on to what we were doing. He confronted us in a meeting one night after hours and said he was going to report us. We offered to cut him in, but that's not what he wanted. Things got heated and he took a swing. One of us, it doesn't matter which one, swung back. Collier fell and hit his head on a coffin. Just like that he was gone. A man was dead, and we were all guilty. You can believe me or not, and if you don't, I don't blame you, but that's the way it happened. It wasn't so much murder as an accident, but he was still dead. And taking responsibility for that wouldn't bring him back.

So, we cremated the body and made it look like Collier had stolen from us and run away. We even sent the family a postcard from abroad to maintain the illusion that he was still alive. I feel worst of all about that, making his family suffer without knowing what really happened to him.

We three pledged ourselves to each other as blood brothers, steeped as we were in Collier's blood, and agreed to take care of each other financially upon our deaths. Clay, who was the sharpest with money and liked to tell us what to do, said it would be better to set it up in the form of insurance so no family members could take it to court as they might with a will. We already had a little bit of partner insurance, so we upped the amount even though it was already clear the business was going south. Ira no longer had the heart for the red market after what we'd done to Collier. If one of us turned the others in, probably guilt-ridden Ira, then the others would cancel the insurance and he'd lose out big-time. That seemed like real insurance to me.

But it's been a few years now and I'm starting to wonder, what if Ira or Clay gets greedy and tired of waiting for me to die? Probably Clay. And if you're reading this, an autopsy must have shown that's what happened. So I'm leaving this along with proof of what we did—Collier's wallet, which the others don't know I have—so that at least my murder won't go unpunished.

If that happens, and this letter becomes public, then maybe the contents will give Collier's family some closure. I hope so. And if nobody ever reads this, well, I feel better having written this confession.

I'm 65 years old, the normal retirement age, so who knows how much time I have left even if one of my former partners doesn't decide to hasten me on my way. I'll try to use the time to make up in some small way for what I've done. Maybe one of the young magicians I am mentoring will make a positive difference in the world.

—   *the late Septimus Pogue*

Chapter Twenty-One
After the Magic

"RUNNING WAS THE gesture of a hopeless man," Mac said a few days later. "And a foolish one as well."

"I'll say!" I agreed. "That was like a confession. He could have bluffed his way out of it, claimed he never saw that fireproof box before."

"But it must have been covered with his fingerprints, darling," Lynda said.

"Oh."

"And perhaps you have forgotten that he shouted 'that's mine,'" Mac piled on.

This was over drinks and dinner with Lexi Pogue and Jack Tanner at Bobbie McGee's. Lynda and Kate filled out the table.

The headline **DRAMATIC ARREST IN POGUE MURDER** had been followed by increasingly smaller headlines in the *Erin Observer & News-Ledger*, but it was still page-one stuff. Belmont was out on bail and insisted he expected to be sworn into the city council on December 1.

"Well, anyway," I came back, "stealing the trunk isn't a straight line to killing Septimus Pogue. The two didn't have to be related. In fact, I'm pretty sure Alfred Hitchcock would call the trunk a MacGuffin."

"Right you are, Jefferson!" Somehow Mac sounded triumphant in acknowledging my point. "The letter in the box only 'convicted' the so-called blood brothers of their long-ago crimes. It really had nothing to do with Septimus's murder other than the fact that the shared secret is what led to the ultimately fatal insurance tontine. You will note that the late Clayton Belmont told the truth about their blood brotherhood, just not all of the truth. I will also point out that Ira Brown's muttered words heard by Rabbi Goldman as Mr. Brown lay dying were undoubtedly 'red market,' the illegal sale of human organs,[14] and not 'red markets' in reference to a game about zombies."

"I still can't believe what Granddad did," Lexi said, the New York strip steak on her plate untouched. Her fiancé put his arm around her. "It's like everything I know about him was a lie, or that he was two different people."

"We're all more than one person," Lynda said. I don't know if that came out of her journalism, her podcasting, or her novel writing—or maybe her strange childhood as the daughter of a world-famous model and a military officer—but it caused me to take her hand in mine under the table.

"All of us have sinned and fallen short of the glory of God," Mac pontificated. Somehow that sounded familiar. "Still, it is always disconcerting to find that a hero's halo is askew."

"Maybe there's a dark side to Damon Devlin as well," Kate said with a twinkle in her green eyes.

Mac was spared from responding when Jack Tanner asked:

---

[14] As I originally interpreted it in conversation with the rabbi. See Ch. 11.—*S. McC.*

"Given that all the stuff that happened more than thirty years ago had nothing to do with the murder of Lexi's grandfather, why did Belmont steal the box with the letter?"

"Probably to spare his father's reputation," Mac said.

"And his own," I threw in. "It wouldn't exactly be good for his business as a financial advisor to be the son of a murderer who illegally sold body parts. Still, that was a misstep. Belmont might have to admit to the theft while pleading 'not guilty' to the murder." And, in fact, that's what he did, although it took some time before his line of defense on the latter charge became clear.

"How did he know where to find the box?" Lynda wondered.

"The only way to know for certain is a confession from Roger Belmont, which seems unlikely," Mac said. "However, Frank Woodford's front-page column about Septimus quoted me as talking about inheriting the magician's trunk. If Septimus told his former partners that he was leaving the letter to me, it would be an easy leap to postulate that it was contained in that trunk. Mr. Belmont could not know the whereabouts of the trunk, of course, but the abandoned Magic Unlimited would be a good place to start—far less risky than trying to break into Septimus's unoccupied home in a residential neighborhood."

"Why do you think he kept the box once he had it?" Lexi asked.

"I suspect that he was piqued at not being able to open it and find out what was inside," Mac said. "Perhaps he kept trying numbers."

"Well, it's a good thing you got the combination right that night on stage at Magic Unlimited. Otherwise, the big reveal would have been a bit of a fizzle."

Mac had the good grace to look embarrassed. "I must concede that I did not leave that to chance, Alexandra. I tried it out in advance. If I had had no clue to the four digits, I would have attempted 1776 for patriotism; 1931, the year Septimus was born; 1941, the year he saw the Great Blackstone perform; 1989, the year Stephen Collier died; and 1990, the year Septimus started the magic shop. However, the phrase 'Sherlockian that you are' in his letter told me that it had to be either 1895 or 2212 for 221B, the master's address on Baker Street."

"Back to the murder," Lynda said. "Why didn't Belmont just put a pillow over his face?"

That question had come up early on, before we knew who the killer was, with no conclusion reached at the time.

"Perhaps lack of strength, given his medical problems," Mac said, "or perhaps he thought it posed less risk of exposure—the injection into the line would have taken mere seconds."

"At least Granddad went peacefully," Lexi said. "There is some comfort in that."

"THAT WAS KIND of painful," I told Lynda later that night, after paying handsomely to ransom our kids back from babysitter Lily Inouye.

"Yeah, poor Lexi," she said.

"Why do murderers in this town always think they can get away with it?" I mused. "Don't they read my books?"

"Or at least listen to my podcasts!"

After a laugh over that, Lynda said:

"The whole magic thing would make this a great case for *Midwest Murders*." That's Lynda's favorite so-called reality show, a must-watch for her every Thursday night on Cincinnati's Channel 11, right before the news (*Live@11 on TV11!*). It's a syndicated show done cheaply, but Lynda doesn't seem to mind. She's suggested several of Mac's cases as grist for their mill, to no avail so far. "They could even re-enact your dark-of-night encounter with a witch while you were exploring Magic Unlimited. Quant would probably go along. And Lexi would make a very dramatic presence on the screen."

"Great idea," I said. "You should shoot them an email and suggest it."

She did so. And that's what led to the second murder involving the magician's trunk.

Part Two

Chapter One
Reality TV

"I CAN'T BELIEVE that *Midwest Murders* is really coming to Erin!" Lynda gushed over Thanksgiving dinner with the McCabes. I was less enthusiastic, not sharing Lynda's fondness for chief correspondent Brock Dandridge, whose wavy hair and bulging muscles were as improbable as his name.

The big news had landed just the day before, via a call from the show's producer to Mac, who immediately called me to say:

"They want to interview me, Jefferson—and you and several other key *dramatis personae*, of course—and re-enact the finding of the magician's trunk at the Lyceum, in which Brian will have a starring role."

How typical! How corny! But there was a bright side, it occurred to me during that Turkey Day dinner.

"If I can finish my account of the Pogue murder and get it into print before the episode airs, the publicity might sell a few books," I said between bites of Lynda's amazing green bean casserole.

"What are you calling this one?" asked Amanda, the middle McCabe child, now 22. I was sure she was going to invent time travel after she finished writing her opera,[15] but pursuing a combined Ph.D./M.D. at the University of Cincinnati is impressive enough.

"*The Magician's Trunk*," I informed her.

"Kind of obvious," opined ginger-haired Rebecca, almost two years older and a graphic designer.

"I like it," the estimable Brian chimed in.

"The case hasn't even gone to trial," Kate pointed out, forever the big sister. "Aren't you afraid of libeling Belmont if he gets acquitted?"

Obviously, her strength is art, not law.

"The truth is a complete defense in American libel law," Mac informed her. "A factual report that a person made an accusation is not libelous, even if the accusation itself is libelous."

If Kate realized this meant her husband was on the hook and not me, she didn't say so.

None of Mac's many previous accusations of guilt in murder cases had gone catawampus in the end, although it had been a near thing once or twice when his preliminary conclusion proved wrong. But there's always a first time. Roger Belmont was still claiming innocence and insisting that he would be sworn into city council the following week with the other newly elected and re-elected members. The usually reliable Erin rumor mill had it that Trudi Belmont was using family money to hire a private eye to supplement the efforts of her husband's defense attorney, the indomitable hell-on-stiletto-heels Erica Slade. No surprise that Erica was taking the high-profile case herself, and not Sally Fair or one of her other protégés. Slade's ex, county prosecutor Marvin Slade,

---

[15] See *Death Masque* (MX Publishing, 2018).

would be leading the other side. I wish I could sell tickets and popcorn for that battle. Belmont insisted the man on the surveillance video entering Elysian Gardens on the day of the murder dressed in FedEx blue wasn't him, but I figured some fancy facial recognition ID software would say otherwise.

The weeks following Belmont's bizarre arrest had been busy ones for the Codys and the McCabes. I wrote most of what regrettably turned out to be only Part One of this account, dealt with the positives and negatives of SBU taking over the failing but asset-rich Licking Falls University about an hour's drive from Erin, and convinced our president, Grant Kingsley, to sit for an interview about the acquisition with the pompous Tony Lampwicke for his stuffy *Crosscurrents* radio program on campus station WIJC-FM. Lynda Teal Cody, Storyteller (as her business card reads) made a true crime podcast of the Pogue business (creatively titled *The Dying Magician Murder*) and worked on the final chapters of her newspaper novel *Ink*. Kate illustrated a children's book for a new author. And Mac, showing his proficiency as a juggler, finished his latest new Damon Devlin mystery while teaching an undergraduate class on "God in Graphic Novels" and rehearsing in the evening for his starring role in the Lyceum Players' mid-December production of *The Man Who Came to Dinner.*

"It's quite an appropriate production for our community, old boy, given that it takes place in a small Ohio town," Mac assured me when the committee of five Lyceum Players chose the classic Moss Hart and George S. Kaufman comedy as its 2023 Holiday Season production.

You may be familiar with the plotline: Critic Sheridan Whiteside, a character based on the real-life radio wit Alexander Woollcott, visits a prominent Ohio family as a publicity stunt, but slips and injures his hip before he even gets into the house. Hijinks ensue as the immobilized "Sherry" takes over the house—and the household—for the next month in his eccentric, egotistical, domineering, and insulting way. It would be unfair to suggest that Sebastian McCabe was a natural for the role; he is seldom insulting. There is no denying, however, that he fits the physical description given in the script—"portly and Falstaffian."

The day after Thanksgiving, I dropped by the theater to see how the sausage was being made. The rehearsal was already underway when I arrived. Trixie LaBelle, in the key role of Whiteside's secretary Maggie Cutler, was saying:

"That was Mr. Stanley's sister, Harriet. I've talked to her a few times—she's quite strange."

"Strange?" responded Mac as Whiteside. "She's right out of *The Hound of the Baskervilles.*" He must have loved delivering that line.[16] "You know, I've seen that face somewhere."

"Nonsense," Trixie/Maggie retorted as she set packages on a table. "You couldn't have."

Trixie may sound like the name of somebody who makes a living taking her clothes off, but actually she makes a living making other people take some of *their* clothes off—she's a urologist. In fact, she's my urologist, acquired when I developed kidney stones some years ago. Trixie is also a fair actress. Not that Lafcadio Figg, who is something of a ham even when not in the theater, was satisfied.

---

[16] Indeed, I did!—*S. McC.*

"Try that again, both of you," he instructed in his Great Director voice. "Sebastian, put more venom in that *Baskervilles* quip and more rumination in the 'seen that face before.' Dr. LaBelle, be more abrupt in your retort. Remember, you've been working for Whiteside ten years—you're the one person in the world he doesn't intimidate."

They tried it again, knowing full well that it would take less time doing so than arguing for the sake of their art. In this halting fashion the rehearsal proceeded for a couple more hours.

By the second scene of the first act, Maggie and newspaperman Bert Jefferson, played by The Bull's Eye shooting range manager Grady Sanders, are mutually besotted. Whiteside knows full well that he is in danger of losing his invaluable secretary as she spends more and more time with her small-town suitor. "I have not even been able to reach you, not knowing what haylofts you frequent," he snarks at one point. The act ends with Whiteside hatching a plot to save his comfortable life by luring a beautiful stage actress to town and, he hopes, into the arms of budding playwright Bert— thus derailing the Maggie-Bert romance.

"That will be enough for today," Figg announced. "I think we are coming along quite nicely. Go home, rest up, and be back at seven sharp tomorrow. Oh, Sebastian—may I have a word?"

"Have I any choice?" Mac rumbled as the other actors and stage crew drifted away.

Figg ignored the rhetorical question. "Speaking as president of the Lyceum Players and the catalyst for saving this fine old theater, I look forward to welcoming that television program to these environs and to our re-enactment of that fortuitous finding of the Blackstone trunk," he said. I found out later that he'd previously given a little speech to his troupe about that coming onslaught, assuring them they that would work their final rehearsals around it.

"I am happy to hear that," Mac assured him.

"And I want to take this opportunity to stress to you that I remain interested in something that was contained therein."

Mac lifted an eyebrow. "Perhaps the crystal ball used by Professor Carlo Stuarti, the original Count of Conjuring himself?"

He was toying with his old frenemy.

Figg took a breath, steadying himself. "I refer, of course, to those vintage baseball cards."

I recalled with disdain that scene at the memorial service when Figg had tastelessly approached Lexi about what he called "those ephemeral icons of sports history," the cards Pogue had used in his act. That was before any of us knew that they were in the trunk, and therefore part of Mac's legacy from his old friend.

"Perhaps once the television crew has come and gone—" Figg went on.

Mac cut him off. "Impossible, Lafcadio! The trunk might feature in the murder trial, and I therefore feel a responsibility to leave the contents intact. And even after that, when I am finally free to dispose of the contents, Mr. Palmer of the Balls & Strikes baseball memorabilia store has shown some interest in those cards—should I decide to sell them, which I surely will not do with the trunk's sentiment-laden exemplars of magical apparatus."

"Nonsense!" Figg exploded, with some justification. "That's just pure pique on your part, Sebastian! I asked about those cards first."

Mac stiffened his spine. "Perhaps Mr. Palmer asked more nicely."

"Ray Palmer is one of my readers," I put in to lighten the mood.

"Who's the other one?" Figg fired back.

I WAS BACK at the theater, with Lynda in tow, two and a half weeks later for the *Midwest Murders* re-enactment of Brian's discovery of the stolen trunk. Word from Mac was that they were doing so in late afternoon immediately upon arriving in Erin so as to interfere as little as possible with final rehearsals for the play, set to open just two days later—at 7:30 P.M. Thursday, Dec. 14. Tuesday's rehearsal was moved to the morning, with the actors adjusting their day job work schedules, where possible, to accommodate.

After taping the trunk scene at the theater, the TV team would then record the necessary interviews of all the key players in the Pogue case—such as Oscar and the Pogues, if they cooperated—over the following days. There was a general feeling of excitement about that in Erin, despite the fact that the last time a reality show came to town that didn't end well.[17] Political types didn't necessarily share that thrill, however; more about that later.

Lynda was smartly dressed in grey-and-black checked slacks, an admirably form-fitting black turtleneck, hoop earrings, a silver necklace, and three-inch heels. Myrtle White

---

[17] See *No Ghosts Need Apply* (MX Publishing, 2021).

had done up her golden hair in a chignon. She scrutinized my hair. "I should give you a trim before you get on camera."

"If you say so." Lynda has been cutting my hair with home clippers for years, at a net savings of thousands of dollars. "I suppose you can't wait to meet that Brock Dandridge guy."

"Oh, didn't I tell you? Word is that Brock's out for the next season, which is in production now, but nobody's saying why—except, of course, people who don't actually know why."

"I see."

Local and Cincinnati media showed up for the filming of the re-enactment, lured there by Figg in search of publicity for the Lyceum Theater and *The Man Who Came to Dinner.* The *Erin Observer & News-Ledger* sent Hadley Reams, who covers education but also writes features, and photographer Imogene (accent on the "I") Casey, who always looks like she should be smoking a cigarette and cussing. Hadley had come a long way from when he was a reporter at the *Spectator,* our student paper, some years earlier.[18] Then he was a skinny kid dressed in jeans, a white shirt hanging out, and a trilby hat. Now he doesn't wear a hat. Imogene was chatting up veteran reporter Kit Atherton from Cincinnati's Channel 11.

"How long are we going to have to wait?" Hadley wanted to know as we milled around in the auditorium. The stage was lit but empty.

"Patience is a virtue," advised Mac, who was decked out in a bow tie as always, this one of grey, blue, and purple.

---

[18] See, for example, *Bookmarked for Murder* (MX Publishing, 2015).

He had met with the *Midwest Murders* crew upon their arrival in town and promised me a pleasant surprise in connection with them, the nature of which he refused to even hint at. Apparently, though, it had nothing to do with Brock Dandridge.

"There they are!" Lynda squeezed my arm.

I could see that. A ponytailed guy and a fair-haired woman about my age were walking toward us, the man carrying video equipment. Before I could register any more than that, the woman yelled "Jeff" and started running my way. By the time she threw her arms around me and kissed me on the cheek, I'd figured out who she was, and I hugged her back tightly. But I couldn't say anything without blubbering so I didn't say anything. Mac insists my eyes were wet; maybe that's why everything got wavy.

It seemed a long time before my beloved spouse made a production number out of loudly clearing her throat before saying, "Hi, there, I'm Lynda Cody—Jeff's wife."

"Then you're a lucky lady," said the other woman, releasing me to address Lynda.

"How true. And you would be...?" She sounded a little tense to me.

You might think I would be terrified, but this was actually kind of fun.

"Oh, I'm Tina Cody. Jeff's cousin."

Chapter Two
The Magician's Trunk Again

"I'VE HEARD OF you!" Lynda exclaimed.

Tina beamed. "Mostly good, I hope."

"Only good, but all childhood and high school memories. You haven't seen each other in like, forever, right?"

"Well, yeah, Jeff and I were in high school when my family left Virginia."

"Until then we were almost like siblings, except for the rivalry part," I said.

"We wrote each other a lot for a while…"

"Then we got busy with college and careers and spouses…"

"And we lost touch. Just one of those things."

After a couple of decades apart, here we were finishing each other's sentences. Did you know that second cousins can marry in all 50 states? I looked that up once. But that was a long, long time ago.

Tina put her arm around me again. She's not as tall as Lynda. "But I've read all your books, Jeff." She always called me Jeff, although to Kate and many other family members I'm known as T.J. "I was thrilled when I found out this was my first assignment for *Midwest Murders*. How's Kate?"

"Still Kate, but less so."

Her chuckle told me that she knew what I meant. Presumably Kate already knew from Mac about Tina's arrival in town, but she was teaching a night-school class at that moment.

"I hate to break up this family reunion," said the ponytailed videographer, clearly not meaning it, "but let's get moving. Who's in charge here?"

"This is my colleague, Tyler Garrett," Tina introduced him, keeping it neutral. Garrett nodded in the general direction of all assembled, not wasting any charm on it. He was shorter than my six-one, but not by much, and reasonably fit. His ponytail was a short one, like my namesake Thomas Jefferson or one of those guys, and he affected the three-day beard look which Lynda likes and I have never understood.

"I suppose you might say that I am in charge here," Figg said, elbowing his way forward. "I am Lafcadio Figg."

And why the hell should I care? said the look on Garrett's face.

"I am president of the Lyceum Players," Figg added.

"And I am Sebastian McCabe," said that worthy with a certain majestic splendor.

Tina, who had merely nodded at Figg, gave Mac a vigorous handshake. "Very pleased to meet you. I've read so much about you. And, of course, you're the star of what's going to be a great episode of our show."

"Hardly the star, Ms. Cody."

"Tina."

"As you wish. I trust that your production will give Chief Hummel and his officers full credit where it is due." Mac's attempts at modesty are always painful, and this was no exception. Humble is not one of the five foreign languages in which he is fluent.

Meanwhile, the videographer Garrett fiddled with his equipment. And by the time Tina had made small talk with what Mac would call the major *dramatis personae*, plus the local press and TV news, he was ready to shoot. The trunk was ready for him, and so was Brian—who'd even combed his hair. We all moved backstage.

"Try to act naturally," Tina advised my nephew (who, come to think of it, was her second cousin once removed). "Pretend this is happening for the first time."

Brian didn't really need coaching to play himself, but he was kind enough not to say so. What ensued wasn't particularly dramatic, although I'd seen enough of *Midwest Murders* to know that a voice-over (now Tina's voice instead of Brock Dandridge's) would milk the scene for suspense. Brian entered a part of the backstage area filled with detritus from previous productions—an old-fashioned telephone here, a jukebox there. He looked around in search of a hammer, spotted the trunk, and took a picture of it with his phone. Then he left.

"That was it?" Tina asked Brian.

"Yeah."

"You didn't open it."

"No. I just texted a picture to my dad. I knew he was looking for it."

"Okay." She turned to Garrett. "Let's get him saying that, with the trunk in the background."

Tina got Brian to expound on his account a bit for the camera, then Mac and Figg re-enacted their banter on the day of finding the trunk, with me standing on the fringes as I had in real life. I like to think I was eye candy.

It went like this:

"Are you sure it's the trunk you're looking for?" Figg asked.

"Quite confident, Lafcadio. This is the Blackstone Senior trunk that was stolen from Magic Unlimited. The real question is, what is it doing here?"

"How should I know?"

Mac looked at Tina. "At this point, I am afraid the following discussion would be quite unedifying to the viewer."

"What's that mean in English?" Garrett asked before Tina had a chance.

"He means he wants to skip to the chase," I said. *Leaving out, for example, that unpleasantness where I suggested that maybe Figg stole the trunk—"purloined" was Figg's word—in hopes of getting his hands on Pogue's baseball cards.*

"Yes, perhaps that would be best," Figg said, as if making a concession. "Much of what was said that day was irrelevant to later events."

The look on Tina's pretty face suggested she knew what was really going on—that is, neither of the big egos thought it was in their best interest to spend time on what proved to be the dry hole of suspecting Figg—but she said: "I'll trust your judgement on that."

Mac ran with it:

"What happened next of significant import was that Brian suggested opening the trunk, but Lafcadio said that would be inappropriate and perhaps illegal for me to do so since the will had not yet gone through the legal formalities. Therefore, I called Alexandra for her permission in her role as executor of the estate. As an aside, Lafcadio was completely in error, and I only called Alexandra to placate him. There was no reason we could not have opened the trunk with impunity."

"That's—" Figg interrupted.

"However, let us move on."

"Yeah, let's!" Garrett said.

So Mac, Figg, and Brian re-enacted their expurgated account of what happened, starting when Brian said: "We can open it and find out. The latch is open, so it's not locked."

When it got to the part where Mac called Lexi Pogue for her permission to open the trunk, she was actually on the other end as arranged in advance. "Put me on Facebook Video so I can watch," Lexi said. As a performer in much of her real life, she made it sound spontaneous. Then Mac handed the phone to Brian and opened the trunk.

That's where it got a little surreal for me. Imogene Casey of the *Observer* and Kit Atherton of Channel 11 shot photos and video, respectively, of Tyler Garrett shooting video. So what we had here was journalists recording for their audience somebody making a recording. Garrett actually shot down into the trunk for a good view of the contents which Mac had left untouched since getting possession of it.

Then the *Midwest Murders* duo spent half an hour or so with Mac, Figg, and me. They'd be talking to Mac much more later, but they wanted to get some footage (if they still call it that) with the Lyceum backstage as a backdrop. Some highlights:

Mac: "Well, yes, to be candid I was a bit surprised at the contents, although I was not shocked that they were highly personal to me and Septimus. More startling, however, was what was missing—a fireproof box that Septimus mentioned in his letter to me from beyond the grave. The insurance policies? Well, they certainly did capture my attention."

Figg: "I knew I hadn't put the trunk there, and I couldn't believe any of our actors had. We think that Belmont—. (*Starts over*) We think the killer must have been dressed as a delivery man or something of the sort, as he was for the murder, to get backstage. Let me assure you that security has tightened since." (This was, to be kind, inaccurate.)

Jeff: "Surprised? Well, I didn't exactly expect the trunk to contain a top hat, a crystal ball, baseball cards, handcuffs, and a fake thumb used by magicians to make things appear and disappear, but I've been around Sebastian McCabe long enough not to be surprised by much of anything."

"You were wonderful, darling!" Lynda assured me with journalistic objectivity after I'd done my turn.

By the time shooting was finished it was about eight o'clock and I was hungry. I helped Mac load the Blackstone trunk into his ginormous Chevy (a trunk in a trunk!).

"Dinner at Bobbie's? I suggested.

Within 10 minutes Mac, Lynda, Tina, and I had a table at Erin's favorite sports bar, with room for Kate when she had finished her class. Bobbie McGee herself—an ace businesswoman hiding under a cowboy hat—took our drink orders, as she is wont to do. That's part of the charm of the place.

"How are you feeling about the first day?" I asked Tina.

"We're off to a good start," she judged.

"I can't wait to see it all come together in the episode!" Lynda said.

"That will take a few months. As you probably know from watching, we like to wait until the trial is over. Then we'll come back for maybe one more day of shooting."

Our drinks arrived, and so did Kate. Massive hugs and kisses between her and Tina ensued, although those two were never as close as Tina and me. I'm told that we siblings look a lot alike, but I think that's just because of the red hair, our reasonably slim body types, and our height. Kate has a lot more hair and it's usually piled on top of her head.

"Where's your videographer?" she asked Tina somewhere into our first drinks.

"Safely elsewhere—safe for me, anyway."

"Don't you two get along?"

My cousin frowned a cute frown. "Not as much as Tyler would like. He wouldn't take 'married' for an answer until I was forced to take action. I kind of think that sort of behavior is why he's paying alimony to an ex-wife."

"I can't believe that kind of crap still goes on," Kate asserted, not quietly. But then she shook her head. "Who am I kidding? We all know it does."

Mac and I, quite prudently, didn't say anything. My mind was back on SBU's biggest sexual harassment mess, which was rather definitely resolved by murder,[19] but I could just as easily have been thinking about the almost-weekly stories in the *Wall Street Journal* about top execs being ousted (usually with golden parachutes) over "inappropriate" or "undisclosed" relationships with subordinates.

"He didn't get physical," Tina clarified, "but his repeated unsubtle comments about my body shape and appear-

---

[19] See *Too Many Clues* (MX Publishing, 2019).

ance were textbook 'unwanted advances.' I lodged a complaint with HR the week after I joined the show. They put a letter in his file and made him apologize." She gave a smirky smile. "That didn't quite satisfy me, so I had Ross—that's my husband—drop by the office one day so I could introduce them. I'm pretty sure Tyler got the point, based on his polite coolness to me since. Still, I insisted that he be booked into a different hotel on this trip."

Tina took a healthy sip of her Cosmopolitan as if to wash the taste of that subject out of her mouth.

"How did you get the job at *Midwest Murders?*" Lynda asked, moving on to more pleasant matters. And with that the two women were off and running, talking about their respective careers. They really seemed to be bonding, and then Tina asked:

"Did Jeff ever tell you about taking me to his junior prom, right before my family moved?"

"No! Please dish!"

"I remember that!" Kate said with a malicious grin. *Thanks, Sis.*

Mac raised an eyebrow.

"I don't really think this is the time—" I began.

"He was just trying to make some girl jealous. But when I talked to her in the ladies' room, it turned out that she was only there with some other guy to make Jeff jealous. And that guy was a hunk! So, we plotted and schemed and by the end of the evening we swapped dates. I really got the better end of the deal, in my opinion."

"I'm sure Lynda finds this ancient history boring, Tina," I said.

"Oh, no. I'm fascinated. Please go on."

"Before that, in the eleventh grade, Jeff was bedazzled by this girl named Wendy Kotzwinkle . . . "

And so forth.

Chapter Three
Bad Publicity

THE LOCAL PAGE of the next day's *Observer* was dominated by Imogene Casey's photo of Tyler Garrett shooting down inside the trunk as if from Mac's perspective when he first looked into it. The photo took up three columns out of four, with Hadley Reams's story (**HIT SHOW IN ERIN**) wrapped around it. A sampling of excerpts:

> The new host of the popular reality crime show *Midwest Murders* arrived in Erin on Tuesday to begin recording an episode about the murder of magician Septimus Pogue.
>
> "I'm excited to be working on my first episode, especially such a fascinating case with so many twists and turns, and one that's recent," said Tina Cody. She replaces former host Brock Dandridge in the season that begins airing next year.
>
> Cody and videographer Tyler Garrett spent their first afternoon re-enacting the discovery of a missing magician's trunk at the Lyceum Theater. The trunk was stolen . . .

The *Midwest Murders* crew also conducted preliminary interviews with St. Benignus University professor Sebastian McCabe, who produced the theory under which City Councilmember Roger Belmont is being prosecuted for the murder; McCabe's son, Brian McCabe, who found the stolen trunk; Lafcadio Figg, president of the amateur theatrical group Lyceum Players; Jeff Cody . . .

And what will happen to the trunk now?

"Septimus willed it to me, and I plan to keep it as a constant memory of him and of our friendship," McCabe said. "I may dispose of some of the contents after the trial to parties who have expressed an interest."

"Hadley should have mentioned that you're Tina Cody's cousin," Lynda opined while pouring breakfast cereal.

"That's not relevant, is it?" Maybe I'm a little defensive of Reams because I took him under my wing a bit when he was a student reporter at SBU.

"Not really, but readers will wonder because the last names are the same, and it's a reporter's job to figure out the readers' questions and answer them. That's basic. Or it used to be. Heck, last week I read a long profile about a national labor leader, and it didn't even give his salary. That's one of the first things I wondered." The sad state of 21st-century journalism is a frequent topic on both sides of the Cody breakfast table. "Anyway, other than that, Hadley's piece isn't a bad story. It's accurate about what happened yesterday, not quite as fawning as what Channel 11 aired last night—"

"Which was blatant promotion of *Midwest Murders*, a show airing on their station," I noted, getting into the spirit of it.

"—and Hadley didn't forget to include Belmont's protestations of innocence, although he did wait until the fifteenth paragraph."

"I wonder how Belmont is managing on city council with the murder rap hanging over his head," I mused.

"Well, council meets today. Why don't you stop by and find out? I'm sure you can think of a work-related excuse. Sam, don't play with your food."

WITH FALL SEMESTER wrapping up at the end of the week, and no PR fires to put out, Popcorn gave me permission to scoot over to our antebellum City Hall in the afternoon. Council meetings are open to the public, with our elected officials sitting in front of microphones at a dais. Only after I grabbed a seat did I realize that somebody was blocking my view—Zoraida Quant! Riley St. James had told me she'd been highly active with videos on TikTok since her losing council bid. I moved to a different seat.

There didn't seem to be any major action items on the agenda, but there were plenty of opinions.

". . . bad publicity," Loretta Danby was saying as I reseated myself. "Everybody who sees *Midwest Murders* is going to think Erin is some kind of homicide haven. I mean, it's just inevitable they're going to regurgitate"—*nice image!*—"McCabe's previous escapades with killers. There's no way you can make lemonade of that lemon."

The 40-something Altiora Corp. engineer, an attractive black woman with hair dyed yellow and done up in cornrows, has a well-earned reputation for speaking her mind on and off council. She's one of my favorite politicos, although that's not saying much.

"This conversation is a waste of time," opined Chad Hollings, who has disagreed with Danby on almost everything since they took office together in 2011. "It's not like there's anything we can do about it."

"But we don't have to co-operate," Danby snapped back. "If they want to interview any of us, we should refuse."

"Fat lot of good that will do," said the elephant in the council chambers, Councilman Roger Belmont. "They won't just go away."

I was pretty sure that all eight of the other council members, and the mayor, wanted Belmont to go away, but he was elected, sworn in, and—as Hollings might say—there wasn't much they could do about it.

"The situation does seem intolerable," Reverend Mayor Sutterlee intoned, "and yet I fear that we must tolerate it. Yes, Mr. Garrison?"

Leonidis Garrison, who operates Garrison's Antiques and Collectibles on Main Street in his day job, peered at his fellow council members through wire-rimmed spectacles. Given his stout physique and walrus mustache, I've always thought he looks a little like Teddy Roosevelt but with longer hair. "Bad publicity related to murder is not exactly a new thing for Erin, is it?" He looked out at the audience. If I didn't know better, I'd think he was looking at me. "I mean, there have been books and podcasts about murders here. Lots of them."

He *was* looking at me—which was totally unfair! First of all, I don't do podcasts; that's in Lynda's wheelhouse. And is it our fault that Garrison's wife's brother was murdered under highly dramatic circumstances?[20] You think he'd be glad that Mac unmasked the killer!

"Unless I'm missing something, we're wasting a lot of time here," said Eleanor Parker, another new member of council, who is a CPA.

You're not missing something.

"Does anybody want to make a motion?" The mayor sounded a little exasperated.

No one did. But they kept talking.

AT HOME THAT evening, Lynda made Cincinnati chili (don't ask) and the children behaved reasonably well. We were just settling into the "getting ready for bed" portion of the day when Oscar called.

"Where's Mac?" he asked.

"Am I my brother-in-law's keeper? But since you asked, he's at the final dress rehearsal for *The Man Who Came to Dinner.* Why?"

"He's not answering his cell and there's been a murder.

More bad publicity!

"Who?"

"A guy named Tyler Garrett. He's—"

"I know who he is."

In about 30 seconds we decided that I would join Oscar at the murder scene—the parking lot behind the Witch's Brew store on Mulberry—and text Mac to meet us there. I

---

[20] See *No Ghosts Need Apply* (MX Publishing, 2021).

knew that upon receiving my message Mac would depart the theater immediately, leaving Figg sputtering.

"Don't wait up," I told Lynda. But I knew she would.

DR. ARLENE EPPENSTEINER, who is all of five-one with dark hair and abundant curls, was already there with the EMTs, Oscar, and the other cops when I arrived. Gibbons let me through the crime scene tape to where the late Tyler Garrett was sprawled on the macadam. I looked just enough to see that his pony-tailed head was a bloody mess.

"Hi, Arly."

"Hi, Jeff. Be careful. Hey, maybe you and Mac ought to buy your own forensic suits."

How weird is it that I'm on a bantering, first-name basis with the coroner, and not from knowing her socially? I'm realistic enough to know that she would have asked me where Mac was if Oscar hadn't already told her. She addressed the latter, apparently answering a question he'd asked before my arrival.

"I can tell you informally, Chief, that the deceased hasn't been deceased more than a few hours," she said. "Rigor mortis isn't complete. But even so, it would have already been dark when he died and all the businesses around here were closed by six o'clock. I checked the business hours on the doors."

"How was he killed?" I asked.

"Hit on the head from behind with some sort of blunt object like a club. The killer could have been hidden in that doorway there."

She pointed to the back of the Witch's Brew store.

"The witch phoned it in," Oscar informed me. He wore a car coat and his official hat. "You know, the crazy lady who owns the store. She says she lives nearby, in one of those old row houses on Water Street, and likes to keep an eye on the neighborhood after hours—"

"A few weeks back she interrupted Mac, Lexi, and me making a late-night visit to Magic Unlimited in search of the magician's trunk," I interrupted to remind him.

"Noted. Anyway, what happened was—"

"Good evening, Oscar." That was Mac, arriving somewhat breathlessly from the Lyceum about four blocks away on Broadway.

"Not for Mr. Garrett it isn't, but thanks for dropping by. Here's what happened: His cell shows that he got a message from a burner phone telling him to meet the caller here with his camera for a good story. Said camera is missing. It doesn't take Columbo to figure out that it was a robbery gone wrong. The bad guy only wanted to knock him unconscious, but he hit too hard, or maybe Garrett had a thin skull."

"His wallet is missing?" I asked.

"Well, no. Just the videocam. But it was professional quality, and those things must be worth a lot of dough."

Mac raised an eyebrow. "A robber who had the victim's phone number and lured him here for the exclusive purpose of stealing his video camera?"

"In case you haven't noticed, the number of looneys walking around today is not small. Like I said, the technical term for what happened here is 'robbery gone wrong.'" *I'm pretty sure that's not actually a technical term, Oscar.* "You're overthinking again."

"Then why did you drag Mac away from his rehearsal and me from my happy home?" I demanded.

"Just bowing to the inevitable. We all know you guys are going to get involved. But, believe me, this is just what it looks like."

"SO, WHAT DO you think?" I asked Mac as we walked back to my Beetle. I was parked in front of the old Magic Unlimited shop, which still had the sign up, although most of the merchandise had been removed and sold on EBTH.

The big guy fired up a cigar.

"I think that Tyler Garrett was not slain by a thief who lured him there to steal his video camera. The robbery was a blind to distract our attention from the real motive, whatever that might be. It was misdirection, just as we faced in Septimus's murder with Roger Belmont's pretense to believe that his father was also murdered."

Mac's cell rang. I only caught one end of the conversation that followed, but that was enough.

"Sebastian McCabe here! Yes, Johanna. How did you know? How enterprising of you! The murder is so recent that I cannot possibly say anything meaningful, except that I have every confidence in Chief Hummel and his fine officers to do what they do best." *I think the word for that sentence is "ambiguous."* "Well, if you insist, then, I will have to say that a connection to Septimus's murder hardly seems likely. A robbery gone wrong appears to be the most likely scenario. He did? Well, there you have it."

After a little more of that, undoubtedly leaving Tall Rawls disappointed that he didn't offer an opinion different from that of the Chief, Mac disconnected.

"What was that all about?" I exploded. "You just told her the opposite of what you believe."

"I would prefer to say that I offered a series of statements that, while true, will misdirect the killer as to my line of thought."

"The killer?"

"Even killers read the newspaper, Jefferson."

Chapter Four
The Show Must Go On

IN MID-MORNING the next day Popcorn called my attention to Johanna's story in the *Online Observer*, the internet product which Lynda created in her earlier life as a daily journalist. After the basic facts and quotes from Oscar and Mac, the account read in part:

> "I'm devasted by Tyler's death," said Tina Cody, new host of *Midwest Murders*. "He was a true professional and one of the best in the business. However, as the old expression has it, 'the show must go on.' We will bring in another videographer. And, unless Tyler's camera is recovered, we will reshoot all of his footage."
>
> Cody acknowledged that Garrett's murder will affect the reality show in another way as well.
>
> "Of course, we will cover the discovery and arrest of Tyler's killer as well, making for an even more compelling episode."

"Not to dis your cousin, but her line about their videographer's murder making for good TV was a little cold," Popcorn judged.

"But true."

"Would you say it that way, Mr. Communications Director?"

"No way. And I'd never use a cliché like 'the show must go on,' either. But just between us chickens, Tina wasn't very fond of the dead man. He had, um, boundary issues with female colleagues."

"Really?" Popcorn's green eyes widened. "Details, please!"

Just as I started to expound, my cell rang. Tina was calling. We'd exchanged phone numbers two days earlier, which now seemed so long ago.

"Cody's Carnival, Head Clown speaking," I answered. Popcorn rolled her eyes and stalked out of the office, coffee mug in hand.

"Hi, Jeff. Guess who's in town?"

"You."

"Ross—my husband. He drove up from Nashville as soon as he heard about the murder. My knight in shining armor! I want you to meet him." Ross Childress was a singer and musician of minor note and a few albums. This I knew because I'd looked him up after our foray to Bobbie McGee's the other night, during which Tina had mentioned his name.

"Let's do lunch," I suggested.

"Before that, how about meeting at Mac's office? I'd like to see where the magic happens."

If she meant Mac's amateur sleuthing and not practicing his ludicrous acts of legerdemain, the magic actually happens in his head and is likely to spill out anytime, anywhere. But I've written enough about the office in these reports that I understand why it would be of morbid interest to one who had not encountered the phenomenon in person.

"If you insist," I replied. "I'm sure the great man will be there. It's not like he'd be teaching—he's a full professor. But don't tell anybody I said that."

I gave Tina the directions to Herbert Hall, settled on a time (half an hour later), then called Mac.

"Excellent, Jefferson!" he said when I'd laid it all out for him. "This saves me the trouble of seeking out your charming cousin."

"Seeking her out for what?"

"Why, to ask who would want to kill her videographer, of course."

THE LOOK ON Tina's face when she and her husband came through the door of Mac's office told me that my writing had not fully prepared her for the chaos. She opened her mouth, then closed it again.

"Welcome to my humble working quarters, Ms. Cody," Mac said.

"Tina," she reminded him. "And this is my husband, Ross."

If I were a casting director, I wouldn't have picked Ross Childress for the part of a Nashville singer. He had a hairless face and only slightly shaggy hair. But he did wear jeans and a leather jacket. And he was solidly built, about six feet tall, and not somebody I would pick a fight with if I were the sort to pick fights.

"Good to meet you," he assured Mac and me equally as he pumped our hands with conviction. His own hand was large and calloused, and I wouldn't want to meet with it in the form of a fist.

"We need to get some video here," Tina said. "When we get a videographer, that is. I expect him to arrive tomorrow."

Nice segue to the business of the day, which is—

"Who would want to kill your former videographer?" Mac asked.

Tina didn't bite her lip in thought as Lynda would have.

"Well, he was creepy around women, but not handsy. At least, not with me." *But then, he'd seen Ross.* "So, no motive there, I guess. But why are you asking? Your police chief is calling it a robbery gone wrong."

Mac answered the question with an unrelated question.

"Do you have any idea how the killer obtained your colleague's phone number in order to summon him to the deadly rendezvous point?"

"Very easily. Garrett gave out his business card to practically everybody he walked by, while telling them he was available for anything from weddings to bar mitzvahs on the side." *Just like Lexi Pogue!* "Oh, that reminds me, have you ever heard of this guy?"

Tina handed Mac a business card that said:

Myles O'Rourke
Confidential Investigator

"Put Your Trust in Us"

A phone number with our area code, 937, was on the back, meaning he was local.

"The name is not familiar," Mac said.

"Ditto here," I chipped in, "which is unusual given our hobby of murder."

"Trudi Belmont told me she hired this guy to find evidence of her husband's innocence, so Tyler and I went to see him yesterday," Tina said. "He seemed a little dodgy to me. Claims to be an ex-cop from Michigan. If so, he was the kind who ate too many doughnuts, if you know what I mean."

I was pretty sure the corpulent (his word) Sebastian McCabe knew what she meant. Rather than commenting on that, Mac asked:

"Did Mr. O'Rourke say what line of inquiry he was pursuing?"

"He was pretty coy about naming names, but he kept saying 'follow the money' and talked about how Septimus Pogue's magic collection was worth hundreds of thousands of dollars, or maybe more."

Lexi!

"A thin reed indeed," Mac said.

"Of course, the video of that interview is gone unless we recover Tyler's videocam. The same goes for everything else he shot in town. It's all in the SD card in the camera."

"To whom else did you talk yesterday?"

"The major characters of the drama—three Pogues and Roger and Trudi Belmont."

WALKING BACK TO the mammoth McCabe vehicle by ourselves after a cousinly lunch for four at the Beans & Books coffee house (chosen for local color), Mac spoiled my mellow mood by saying:

"You realize, of course, that Tina must be considered a suspect, given the deceased's amorous intentions toward her."

"What? Don't even joke like that."

"I am not jesting, Jefferson, I assure you."

"The idea is ridiculous. Killing a guy for a few fumbled passes would be overkill."

We climbed into the mammoth car, which ought to have a cool name like "the Red Dragon," but doesn't.

"Perhaps they were completed passes that Tina now regrets," Mac said as he eased out of the parking lane. "She may have understated the situation."

"Bullocks!" I got that from those British mystery shows Lynda likes to watch. "Tina would never do either of those things—murder *or* hanky-panky."

At least, Teen Tina wouldn't. But that was three decades ago.

I plowed on:

"And why would she call her co-worker on a burner phone?"

"Because she knew the number would show up on his cell. Granted, that would not be unusual given that they were colleagues, but the timing would have been suspect."

"Then why not just steal the phone along with the videocam?" I bounced back.

"She wanted to make it look like an unknown person called him. Might not someone associated with a true crime program think that way?"

"You have an answer for everything. Do you really think Tina's a good suspect?"

"A good one? No. I am inclined to think that if Tina Cody had committed the murder and wanted it to look like a robbery, she would have stolen something else, not the video so necessary to her inaugural effort on the program."

"Good point! So, who *would* make a good suspect?"

"We need to approach that in our usual methodical way. Shall you join me in my office?"

"How about if you come to mine for a change?"

"As you wish, Jefferson."

At the Gamble Building, I made Mac cool his heels for twenty minutes or so while I checked in with St. Simon and Link in their lairs just to keep them on their toes. I came back to find him amusing Popcorn with a card trick.

"Don't you have work to do?" I asked her.

"You took the words right out of my mouth, Boss."

Ignoring this insubordination, I stalked into my office and opened up the word processing program. Mac joined me shortly, apparently having finished his trick.

"I suppose this is where we build a chart of suspects, motives, and alibis," I told him.

"I prefer to think of it as a table."

"Semantics!"

"The table should, of course, for the sake of completeness include both your cousin and her husband."

"But Ross just arrived in town this morning!"

"So he says. We unmasked a killer not that long ago who was in town much earlier than it appeared."

"Okay, but if we're going to include them, we have to list Oscar's speculated robber as well. Who else?"

"Lafcadio, of course."

"What possible reason—"

"I concede that I can think of none at the moment. However, we are brainstorming, Jefferson. This is not the time to put up objections to names on the list, which is why I raised no objection to the mythical robber. Who else?"

He knew who else, but he wanted me to say it:

"The Belmonts and the Pogues, just because they're involved in the case that brought Garrett to town. Hey, wait a minute!" I'd had a sudden flash of insight. "Maybe something damaging to one side or the other in the Pogue murder case came up in an interview that Garrett taped with a Belmont or a Pogue—or with Myles O'Rourke, the dodgy private eye. It could have been something so minor that Tina wouldn't even notice it at the time or remember it later, but it showed up on the video that the killer stole. I've had that experience—hearing something on a video that I didn't pay attention to when it was said live in front of me."

"Even more credible would be the notion that Mr. O'Rourke intended to procure information gleaned in those interviews and the effort came a cropper," Mac asserted. "I have asked Colonel Gibbons to see what he can find out about that reputed ex-policeman. However, it seems rather unlikely to me that anyone would be so injudicious as to say something on camera that he would murder to conceal."

"Don't be too sure—I've more than once said something to a reporter that I regretted later, and I'm a pro at talking to media. Anyway, to continue, let's add Zoraida Quant."

"Surely she would not have left the body behind her own building and then alerted the police!"

"That's what she would have expected us to think. Or she was just being her usual crazy self. Works either way."

"Motive?"

"Maybe Garrett didn't like witches. Wait! Even better—she wanted to steal his videocam to improve the quality of her TikTok videos!"

"I scarcely think, Jefferson—"

"We're brainstorming, remember? So, let's also add a generic jealous husband. Maybe Garrett wasn't always as restrained in his advances toward women as he was with Tina."

"Do you posit one so offended that he followed his victim here, or odious actions on Mr. Garrett's part almost immediately after arriving?"

"Whatever. And while we're dealing with spouses, let's not forget that Tina mentioned Garrett had an ex-wife. You know spouses are the most likely killers in everyday homicides."

And that's where I ran out of gas.

"I believe our list is more than comprehensive—it is imaginative," Mac said.

In chart—or table—form it looked like this:

Suspect	Motive	Alibi
Belmonts	Hiding something in interview that could hurt Roger's defense	
Ross Childress	Victim came on to his wife	Supposedly not in town
Tina Cody	See above	
Jealous Husband	See above	
Bitter Ex-Wife	Hatred; psychological satisfaction	
Myles O'Rourke	Bungled attempt to get information	
Pogues	Hiding something in interview that could help Roger's defense	
Robber	Robbery gone wrong	
Zoraida Quant	Robbery gone wrong (or even more bizarre reason)	

"Here we are, then," I said. "But where in the Hades are we?"

"That, Jefferson, is an excellent question, the answer to which eludes me."

Chapter Five
Opening Night

A FEW HOURS later on that Thursday—at 7:30 P.M., to be precise—the curtain went up on *The Man Who Came to Dinner* at the Lyceum Theater.

There's a reason that a play that premiered in New York on October 16, 1939, is still being produced: The situation is inherently funny, and some of the lines are hilarious in context. (STANLEY: "How do you do, Mr. Whiteside? I hope that you are better." WHITESIDE: "Thank you. I am suing you for a hundred and fifty thousand dollars.")

I have to disagree, though, with Henry Knox Wilcox, long-time freelance critic for the *Observer* who hailed "Sebastian McCabe's pitch-perfect performance as Sheridan Whiteside." Mac wasn't acting. He *is* Whiteside, only more polite. I can well imagine him, for example, thinking: "Is there a man in the world who suffers as I do from the gross inadequacies of the human race?" But he wouldn't say it out loud, as Whiteside does in Act One, Scene 1.

With 15 men and nine women in the play, Wilcox couldn't name them all in his review without making it a laundry list. So, I was pleased that he had room to give shout-outs to "the effervescent Ms. Riley St. James" as June Stanley and the "convincingly sincere Brian McCabe" as her brother

Richard. He also favorably mentioned "Lyceum Players veterans" Jonathan Hawes as family patriarch Ernest Stanley and Dr. Trixie LaBelle as Maggie Cutler.

Applause rocked the house when the curtain rang down on (spoiler alert) Whiteside once again being put into a wheelchair after falling a second time at the end of the play. Among the whole-hearted clappers were Mo Russert (married to Jonathan Hawes), former TV anchor Nadine Lattimore, Triple M, Reverend Mayor Sutterlee, Aurelia Banfield with L. Jack Gibbons, Tony Lampwicke, Tall Rawls and not-tall beau Seth Miller, my boss Lesley Saylor-Mackie, and philanthropist and *Observer* owner Serena Mason.

Less enthusiastic, it seemed to me, but still clapping was Ralph Pendergast, president of the Sussex County Convention & Visitors Bureau. Although Ralph often butted heads with Mac and me when he'd been SBU's provost, we now got along reasonably well. But I could see that peace being shattered by Mac taking part in the negative tabloid TV publicity over the Pogue murder, with a woman named Cody as the pretty face of the program.

That was still on my mind when Lynda and I arrived home, received a report on the now-sleeping kids' behavior (and misbehavior) from Lily Inouye, and settled in to watch the last few minutes of a *Midwest Murders* episode recorded months ago with that wavy-haired Brock Dandridge asking the questions and providing the voice-over. It was about a millionaire who disappeared after being accused of murdering his daughter's nanny. Tina's style would be different, no doubt, but "Murder and the Magician" or some such would still be wrapped in sensationalism. Such were my thoughts when Mac called. I assumed he just wanted to process the opening night, or maybe fish for compliments, so I fore-stalled that by answering the phone with:

"Ralph is going to defecate a brick"—I thought Mac would like that—"when the *Midwest Murders* hits the air with Erin portrayed as the murder capital of Ohio."

"Blast it, Jefferson, this is no time to worry about Ralph's petty public relations problems!" Mac roared. "I have been robbed. The magician's trunk is gone again."

Chapter Six
Suspicious Character

"GONE? STOLEN! HOW?"

I was not at my most articulate.

"The miscreant stood on the patio and broke the back kitchen window. The trunk was in my study, where it rested after we finished with it at the Lyceum the other day."

"But the burglar wouldn't know that. He must have nerves of steel to go through the house looking for it with the alarm banging." I'd accidentally set off our home alarm more than once, and I got a headache just thinking of the sound.

I could have counted to ten during the embarrassed pause before Mac said:

"Erm, that was not an issue."

"You mean you didn't set the alarm?" My voice may have risen a bit.

"I was rushed, Jefferson."

"You told me once that you sometimes forget to set the alarm,[21] but this was the worst possible time to be the absent-minded professor. Oscar will never let you live this down."

---

[21] See *Erin Go Bloody* (MX Publishing, 2016).

"It could happen to anybody," Oscar said late on Friday morning as he poured himself a cup of fully caffeinated coffee from his office Keurig machine. He drank deeply, then said: "Just kidding. That was a really dumb thing to do, Mac."

"I think you mean a really dumb thing to *not* do," I said helpfully. "*Not* set the alarm."

"Once again the trunk goes missing in the midst of a murder case, causing us to ponder how the two homicides might be related," Mac mused around his own coffee mug, ignoring our badinage. "In the case of Septimus's murder, the trunk turned out to have only a tangential relation to the crime, that being the fireproof box with the materials related to the shameful and appalling affair that tied the three 'blood brothers' together. It hardly seems likely that this second theft of the trunk has anything to do with the murder of Mr. Garrett. Perhaps it is all about muddying the waters for the case against Roger Belmont!"

"It couldn't be that somebody stole the trunk because—I don't know—maybe because they wanted what was inside?" Oscar said. He is no master of sarcasm, but I have to give him credit for trying. "Just like maybe somebody killed that video guy for his camera, seeing as how the camera was stolen."

Mac ignored that. "The trunk calls attention to the Pogue family, of course."

"And to you," I said.

"Ah, yes. About that. Perhaps it would be best not to make this unfortunate matter public. That might be just what the thief wants us to do."

"That's rich!" Oscar said. "You asking to hush up the burglary. I'm not the publicity hound in this room! By the way, speaking of matters related to Pogues and Belmonts, Gibbons ran down the history on that PI, O'Rourke. He was a cop, all right, in Warren, the third largest city in Michigan. He was fired in 2020 for excessive use of force during an arrest, which led to the suspect suffering a concussion. That's on the record. Off the record, according to a chatty source, he was also on the take."

"Not a nice guy," I observed.

"I hate cops like that. When I was on the Dayton force—"

"*Midwest Murders* are here, Chief." That was Holly Burdette, interrupting from the doorway. "Jeff's cousin and a guy with a camera."

"Oh, great!" Oscar said.

"Your time to shine," I told him. "You should be happy they want to talk to you. You can explain your role in exposing Roger Belmont."

"Show 'em in," he grunted to Holly.

He had barely finished the last word when Tina entered, accompanied by a man who seemed as much weighed down by the world as by his equipment. In age he seemed to be sixty-plus, although that might have been just the effect of the gray hair and the bags under his eyes. What he lacked in height he made up for in weight.

Tina offered a jaunty, "Hello, gentlemen—and Jeff." *Cute, but unoriginal.* "Good to meet you, Chief Hummel. Jeff's told me so much about you." Hands were shaken. "This is my new videographer, Sam Phillips. He does a lot of work for our producer, Kingston Productions—just flew in from a cooking show in San Francisco."

Out of the frying pan . . . As further introductions and handshakes followed, Phillips smiled and became a whole different person; he no longer looked world-weary.

Tina shed her coat, revealing a camel-colored wool blazer over a red blouse and dark pants. "I was hoping to get you on camera here in your office, Chief, talking about the Pogue case and Tyler's murder. And you already know I'd like to get you in your office, too, Mac. Background is important. We're a visual medium."

Oscar looked canny. "Maybe we'd better talk a little first before you start recording. Let's be clear: I'm not going to break any news here. The Pogue case is done and dusted, and I can recap what's public on that. But there's not much I can say about the murder of your co-worker. These are early days on that one."

"Of course. I completely understand."

"Incidentally, whom else have you interviewed this morning?" Mac wondered.

"We caught up with Lexi Pogue. She's afraid that her grandfather's killer will escape justice."

"I fervently pray that he will not!"

"Wait a minute," I said. "I thought you said you interviewed her with Garrett?"

Tina shook her head. "No. Mac asked who I talked to. I *talked* to all the Pogues to try to set up interviews. But Adrian and Sable refused to go on camera, and Lexi couldn't do it until today because of her schedule. Why?"

Because that wipes out the possible motive of one of the Pogues killing Garrett and stealing his video to hide something one of them said during the interview. Maybe Mac was right about the theft being a red herring, a distraction to make us think the murder was about the camera or the contents of its SD card. The expression on his hirsute face said he was thinking the same thing.

"Never mind," I said.

"What about Roger Belmont?" Mac asked. "Did you actually interview him and his wife?"

"We did, not that his lawyer would let him say very much. That Ms. Slade is quite a force of nature! She should have her own show."

What a great idea! I made a mental note to remind Tina of that when this mess was over.

"I arrested Councilman Belmont and charged him with murder," Oscar reminded everybody, in case we forgot. "What happens to him next, my office has no control over. Erica Slade and her ex will duke that out in court and twelve fine citizens of Sussex County will convict or acquit."

"Will you repeat that on camera?" Tina asked.

"No way. I'm not about to mention the slugging Slades on TV."

"Belmont's defense attorney and the county prosecutor used to be married," I told Phillips, answering the question mark on the videographer's face. At this point I could have mentioned Marvin Slade's womanizing that caused his Bengal cheerleader wife to go to divorce court and then law school, but that would have been gossiping. Besides, by this time Phillips was ready to get to work.

"Let's start at the beginning, Chief," Tina said. "When did your office become involved in the death of Septimus Pogue?"

"When our coroner, Dr. Arlene Eppensteiner, determined that it was a homicide. Until then it was just the death of a 92-year-old in a nursing home."

"A man who was so afraid of being murdered that he left instructions to have an autopsy conducted. When did you decide to bring Sebastian McCabe into the case?"

"When he informed me about the coroner's finding."

When the episode aired, months later, the audience was treated at this point to a look of shock on Tina's face. But that was actually filmed later. When there's only one camera, that's how it works.

"You didn't know the coroner's finding until he told you?" Tina asked.

Oscar squirmed. "Well, it wasn't actually official at the time he told me. Look, this wasn't an ordinary situation. The postmortem was done at the request of the family, through Professor McCabe, so Dr. Eppensteiner conveyed the preliminary results to him informally. She quite properly notified our office when she completed her written autopsy report."

"What steps did you take then?"

"We proceeded on several fronts, such as checking the records of the Elysian Gardens—the scene of Mr. Pogue's poisoning—to find out who had visited him before his death."

"And did that turn up the name of anyone you considered a suspect?"

And so forth.

Just when it looked like things were wrapping up, Tina said, "Of course, I have to ask you about your progress in investigating the death of our beloved colleague, Tyler Garrett."

"I'm sure you can understand, Ms. Cody, it's far too early for me to say anything about that other than that the investigation is continuing, and it has our highest priority."

Phillips put down his camera.

"Okay," Tina said, "what gives?"

"Hey, the body's barely cold," Oscar said, shedding his somewhat more formal on-camera manner. "His ex, Shana Garrett, is on her way here to identify it."

The ex-wife! She was on our table of suspects.

"Where's she coming from?" I asked. It wouldn't be the first time in one of our cases that a killer appeared to be out of town at the time of the murder, as Mac had reminded me.

"Salzburg, Austria," he said. "I talked to her there myself. Apparently, the Christmas markets there are a big deal."

"*Christkindlesmarkt* is what they call them in Germany," Tina supplied, "but in Austria they're known as Advent markets. They have them all over the country."

I made a mental note not to tell Lynda about this opportunity to spend thousands of euros.

"Did the ex-widow sound distraught?" Mac asked.

"Hell yes, she did! The dead man was paying her alimony."

BACK AT MY office that afternoon, I fielded a call from journalist Deidre Chandler of the *Cincinnati Sentinel*, an online-only newspaper that made a noble effort to actually do reporting.

After the usual pleasantries, she said: "I'm working on a story about construction at colleges and universities in our area and what that's doing to tuition. SBU, for instance, has that new Bainbridge Building going up."

I'd been expecting this ever since the *Wall Street Journal* ran a front-page story that August under the headline "State Colleges 'Devour' Money, and Students Foot the Bill." It reported how selective public universities across the country had been on a spending spree for two decades, shoveling money into "snazzy academic buildings and dorms" as well as sports programs and administrators, while raising tuition far more than state funding had been cut. Although I felt sorry for my counterparts at the institutions named in the story, it was well-researched and meaningful journalism.

"The entire cost of the Bainbridge Building was paid for by a generous bequest from the late Ezra Bainbridge through his foundation," I was happy to tell her. "And, incidentally, we've been able to hold tuition steady again this year despite the roughly eight percent inflation rate in 2022."

"How did you manage that?" Chandler asked when I took a breath.

"By working at it," I said. "Our president, Grant Kingsley, and the entire administration are dedicated to keeping SBU affordable. That's been a years-long, multipronged effort that included keeping the staff trim." *We also reduced deadweight faculty and programs, but no need to mention that.*

Toward the end of the conversation, I had another call coming in which I ignored. It was Mac, and I called him back.

"You rang?"

"Yes, Jefferson, I am in my office, and I think you will want to join me."

"Does it ever occur to you that I have a day job, and this is daytime?"

"Mr. Ray Palmer is here. He informed me that you visited him during the Pogue murder investigation, which you did not mention to me."

Caught!

"Well, you said you weren't going to sell until the trial was over." *Plus, Palmer shot down my brilliant theory that the cards were hugely valuable and therefore the motive for the Pogue murder.*

"However," Mac plowed on, "that is beside the point now. He has just told me something very interesting that I wanted you to hear first-hand."

I HADN'T SEEN Palmer since that day in October when I'd visited his baseball card shop, Balls & Strikes, without telling Mac. He looked the same, short and solid and still wearing an out-of-season Cincinnati Reds baseball cap.

"Please tell Jefferson what you related to me," Mac said to Palmer.

The shop owner seemed embarrassed. "Well, if you think it will help. Thing is, the stories in the *Observer* about this TV show in town regarding the Pogue murder reminded me that Professor McCabe has those baseball cards he inherited from the victim. They're not extremely valuable, but he's no collector and I'm always in the market for inventory. Anyway, Thursday night I happened to be in the neighborhood of his house at 23 Half Moon Street and—"

"How did you know where he lives?" I asked.

"From your books."

"Oh."

"Anyway, just as I pulled up across the street, I saw a guy hustling into a minivan parked in the McCabe driveway. At first, I thought it was Professor McCabe because he was taller than me and wide but then I realized he didn't have a beard. The guy looked right at me for a few seconds and—maybe it's my imagination—I thought he looked guilty. A real suspicious character, I would say. He drove out of there like a bat out of hell."

"Does the description resonate with you, Jefferson?"

This was a test, and I didn't want to fail it, but I didn't see where he was going.

"An individual of some girth whose name appears on the table we compiled," Mac prodded.

Then I got it.

"Would you say that he looked like a cop who ate too many donuts?" I asked.

Not surprisingly, Palmer looked a bit puzzled.

"Yeah, I guess so. Why?"

"Because we have a strong suspicion that we know who that is," Mac informed him.

Palmer didn't need to know that his name was Myles O'Rourke, the former Warren, Michigan, policeman turned Erin, Ohio, "confidential investigator."

"About those baseball cards," Palmer began.

Chapter Seven
Counsel for the Defense

I'LL SPARE YOU the details of Tina's interview with Mac in his office, which came hard on the heels of Ray Palmer's departure. I sat in for most of it in my official capacity as media liaison for SBU faculty, although I ducked out during part of it to answer some budget questions from Saylor-Mackie. The part that I heard included such standard fare as, "What was the turning point in your investigation?" But there was also the occasional surprise query, such as, "Do you think anyone who wasn't a magician could have seen through the misdirection in this case?" That last prompted Sam Phillips to ask from behind his camera, "Who's solved more mysteries, you or Damon Devlin?" Then he hauled out from his camera bag some books for Mac to sign.

If you want to know the answers to any of those questions, you'll have to watch the episode. Check your local listings or go to the website for streaming info.

After about an hour, only a few minutes of which would appear on the air, the *Midwest Murders* team prepared to leave.

"Incidentally," Mac said to Tina with a casual air, "where were you when your colleague was killed?"

My cousin gave an eyebrow-raise worthy of Sebastian McCabe but only asked, "Has the coroner pinned down the time?"

"I have not read the postmortem report. However, her preliminary conclusion was that it was certainly after dark."

"I'm staying at the Winfield, so I had dinner in their bar, Malarkey's Pub, at about six o'clock or so, after our interview with that O'Rourke guy." There would be a time stamp on the receipt if she paid by credit card, but she probably didn't. She would have put it on her hotel bill. Mac didn't ask her, but I could see him processing that. Tina continued: "Then I had a long Zoom call with Ross, whom I hadn't been with in person for a week, after which I took a cold shower."

The fact that I couldn't tell whether that last part was a joke reminded me that I didn't really know the adult Tina, which was something to keep in mind.

"You're just checking boxes, right?" she asked Mac. "I mean, you're doing the alibi thing."

He bowed slightly. "That is an apt characterization."

Phillips thought it was kind of cool that his co-worker needed an alibi, if I read his face right. He finished packing and the duo soon departed in a cloud of handshakes and a cousinly kiss from Tina for me.

"That was fun," I lied.

"It was necessary," Mac said. "Now for Mr. O'Rourke."

"Don't you have to get ready for the play tonight?"

"Indeed I do, Jefferson. However, we have time to ask a minor player in this little true-life drama a few questions. That will ease my mind and improve my performance."

That sounded like rationalization to me, but I didn't press it. Mac pulled out the O'Rourke business card that Tina had passed on to him the day before. He called the number and put his cell on the speaker.

"Sebastian McCabe here, Mr. O'Rourke!"

"You say that like I ought to know who you are," came the response after a short pause.

"Please do not be coy. I have no time for that, Mr. O'Rourke. You were at my residence last night in my absence."

"According to who?"

That's "whom." But Mac ignored the grammatical error, showing how focused he was.

"Perhaps we should meet in person."

"If you say so. I'm at a joint called Gatsby's. I'll let you buy me a drink or two."

GATSBY'S GASTROPUB AT the corner of High and Front streets, formerly known as The Speakeasy, was the scene of two murders exactly 100 years apart.[22] When we got there, Myles O'Rourke was killing a pint of a dark brew. He was easy to spot, partly because the after-work crowd hadn't gathered yet, and partly because of the body shape that had him squeezed into a booth. Also, he waved us toward him.

"McCabe and his pal Cody," he told us as we joined him, although we knew that. The fact that he knew my name as well as Mac's showed that he'd been briefed by his employer. "You wanted to talk, so talk."

---

[22] See (yet again!) *No Ghosts Need Apply* (MX Publishing, 2021).

O'Rourke had a pug nose, thinning hair, and all the charm of a prizefighter who'd had a few drinks. Which he had.

"What were you doing at my home last night?" Mac asked him.

"I didn't say that I was." He quaffed the last of his beer.

"Nevertheless, you were. And something of great sentimental value to me subsequently disappeared."

"As in stolen," I clarified. "Disappeared" sounded too much like a magic act.

O'Rourke looked from one to the other of us, seemingly surprised, if I read his expression correctly. "Stolen from the house? No shit? Okay, I'll quit clowning around. I tried to pay a call on you—nice digs, by the way—but if somebody robbed the place I sure as hell know nothing about it. Hey, wait! Maybe I do."

But before he could amplify, a young man with a dangling earring came around and took our drink orders—another Queen City Stout for O'Rourke, a Flying Pig Porter for Mac, and Caffeine-Free Diet Coke for me because I was saving myself for cocktail hour with Lynda.

When the server had departed, O'Rourke leaned forward. "Some guy in a Kia was giving me the hairy eyeball when I got back to my car. I couldn't see his face, but he was wearing glasses and a baseball cap."

Ray Palmer. Well, that brought things full circle: Palmer told us about O'Rourke; now O'Rourke was telling us about Palmer. Somehow that seemed like a circular firing squad to me. I was beginning to wish I'd ordered an adult beverage.

"What were you doing at my home?" Mac repeated.

By this time the Queen City Stout was in front of him, and O'Rourke was feeling more co-operative. "I know you're in tight with the local cops, and I'd rather talk to you than them. So here's the score: My client, Trudi Belmont, has a theory that you're the real killer of Septimus Pogue. I was just scoping out the scene, trying to learn whatever I could about you. Getting your vibes, you know?"

"That is the dumbest idea I've ever heard, bar none," I said. *And I work in higher education.* "How does she explain away the video surveillance showing her husband at the nursing home dressed like a delivery man?"

O'Rourke shrugged. "Not my circus, not my monkey, but she says that's not him. Anyway, I could tell that nobody was home from the light being on in the front room—that's always a dead giveaway because people do that when they leave a house."

"Thus, clearing the way for you to break in through the window at the rear of the house," Mac said.

"I didn't do that! I never even got to the back of the house. I heard a neighbor's car pull in the driveway next door and figured I'd better skedaddle before anybody saw me. It seemed like the kind of neighborhood where people would notice."

"Somebody did notice," I said. "The driver of the Kia."

"So that's how you knew I was there?"

Ignoring the question, Mac demanded, "Where were you on Wednesday night?"

"You mean the night that TV guy was killed? I was babysitting my two grandkids. That's why I moved to this

Podunk town. My daughter lives here and her scumbag husband left her for a younger model. She needed help and I was, uh, at liberty, jobwise. Plus, I'm a widower with no attachments back home." O'Rourke downed the second drink. "I think I've said enough, or maybe too much. If you want to know anything else, ask my lawyer—Erica Slade."

"I AM NOT his lawyer," Slade said, her fiery violet eyes wide. Billboards around town show her with her dukes up and boxing gloves on ("I fight for you!"), but today she was garbed for court in a businesslike but upscale midnight-blue dress. "I work for Trudi Belmont, and so does he. That's the extent of our connection. Defense counsels do sometimes employ private detectives, but I didn't do so in this matter."

SladeLaw is housed in a former Episcopal chapel on Water Street, only a few blocks from Gatsby's. The building still has the stained-glass windows from its days as a house of worship and the bar from the brief period it was an eatery called The Sanctuary. Slade, an after-hours friend to Lynda and me despite her propensity for defending killers, had acquired the property from a client in payment of her large fee.

"Trudi must really believe in Roger's innocence," I told her.

"All my clients are innocent—somehow."

"Possibly including whoever killed Tyler Garrett," I quipped.

"The identify of which we are attempting to ferret out," Mac said.

"Good luck with that."

"It has occurred to us as a remote possibility that Mr. Garrett may have been killed because of something harmful to your defense of Roger Belmont that came up in the interview he recorded with you and Mr. Belmont. I do not suppose you have any idea where your client was on Wednesday evening?"

Erica Slade's laugh, though seldom heard, is a delight. "As a matter of fact, Councilman Belmont and Trudi were with me all evening at a fundraiser for Judge Kessler. Hey, I'm going to the play tonight, so break a leg, Mac."

Chapter Eight
Alarm!

IT WAS ANOTHER actor who broke a leg before curtain time—Jenny Lewis—so Kate was pressed into a role that she had played once in our student days at St. Benignus College, as it was then. So, even though we had been at the premier, Lynda and I attended the Friday night performance of *The Man Who Came to Dinner* as a matter of brotherly love. Tina tagged along.

Oscar and Popcorn were also in the audience (holding hands!), along with such familiar faces as both Slades, not holding hands but seeming friendly enough to titillate the gossip mill; Dr. Dante Peter O'Neill, dean of SBU's Rev. Joseph F. Pirelli School of Arts and Humanities; James Hancock Bridges, Jr., veteran attorney and the bluest of local bluebloods; and Dr. Abington with his wife, June, as well as their daughters, Ruth and Naomi.

Kate performed well in the minor part of Harriet Stanley, seen briefly in the first act, who (spoiler alert!) turns out to be an axe murderer.

Lynda grabbed my arm at intermission. "Look!" she whispered. "It's the witch!"

Zoraida Quant, her curly gray hair tinged with blue to match her large glasses, was talking to the only slightly taller

Ray Palmer, whose body language said he was desperately trying to escape her clutches.

"Colorful character," Tina said. "She's the one who walked in on you and Mac in the old magic shop, right? She's on our interview list but I haven't lined her up yet."

"She's on our list, too—the suspect list for Garrett's murder," I said. "Mac doesn't seem to think she has a good motive, but who knows what would cause Zoraida Quant to do anything? Trying to get into her mind is like a voyage into the heart of darkness."

My own mind wandered a bit, to tell the truth, as the second act unfolded. We had a full list of potential suspects and motives for killing Tyler Garrett, and we were slowly filling in the alibis as well. But what if Oscar was right and somebody just wanted Garrett's camera, probably not for what was on the SD card but to resell it for drug money?

Trixie LaBelle's riveting performance near the beginning of the third act pulled me back into the play. Maggie Cutler, Sheridan Whiteside's secretary, is fed up with her scheming boss and she tells him off:

"I think you are a selfish, petty egomaniac who would see his mother burned . . . at the stake . . . if that was the only way he could light his cigarette. I think you'd sacrifice your best friend without a moment's hesitation if he disturbed the sacred routine of your self-centered, paltry little life. I think you are incapable of any human emotion that goes higher up than your stomach, and—"

And the fire alarm went off, an irritating sound accompanied by a recorded voice giving us instructions on how to exit.

The entire audience jumped up and obeyed the directions reasonably well, proceeding calmly and avoiding panic.

"Well, this is memorable," Tina said on our way out.

Sussex County's volunteer fire department is one of the best in the state, and they were soon on the job. After about half an hour of standing in the cold, the fire chief told us we could go back in. When we had done so, Lafcadio Figg appeared on stage.

"Ladies and gentlemen, the show will go on!" he announced, not shunning a slight variation on the obvious cliché.

The play recommenced from the beginning of Maggie's harangue, ending with "—and I was the fool of the world for ever thinking that I could trust you."

By the time the curtain went down on Whiteside's second accident at the Stanley house, the fire alarm had become no more than a story to tell our friends over the weekend.

Lynda and I took Tina back to her hotel, then headed home to find the kids safely asleep and Lily Inouye likewise. We were in the house less than five minutes when my cell rang. It was Mac, and he didn't give me the chance to offer a greeting.

"Blast it, Jefferson, it is back!"

"What's back?"

"That peripatetic magician's trunk. It has reappeared backstage here at the Lyceum."

Chapter Nine
Curtain

WITH CHRISTMAS JUST nine days away, Lynda and I spent most of Saturday Christmas shopping in Cincinnati for things I didn't know we wanted until Lynda saw them. (And that new red kimono looks great on her!) It wasn't exactly a *Christkindlesmarkt*, but satisfactory.

And also on that day, I helped Mac solve the murder of Tyler Garrett.

He called me in the afternoon while I was watching Lynda give our credit card a workout at Kohl's.

"I have a notion about why the magician's trunk was once again stolen and restored," he said, "and if I am correct, the evidence is in your hand at this moment."

He was correct.

But he chose not to do anything about it until he could stage a big reveal after Sunday's 2 P.M. matinee performance of *The Man Who Came to Dinner*, once again showing a flair for the dramatic that was equal parts Sherlock Holmes and David Copperfield.

Although Mac hadn't gone public about the reappearance of the trunk—"Let the killer worry about what I am up to!"—Tina knew and was there on Sunday with Sam Phillips to again record a re-enactment of Brian finding it.

The backstage scene on Sunday wasn't quite what that great philosopher Yogi Berra once called déjà vu all over again. The cast this time was a bit different. Brian, Figg, and Lynda were there, this time along with Kate. But the only representative of local media was Johanna, tipped off by Mac. And Ray Palmer was on hand to stand next to the magician's trunk with the baseball cards inside and talk about seeing a "suspicious character" at Mac's house.

"I had to close up the shop early for this," Palmer groused. I put that down as posturing, since Balls & Strikes didn't seem to be booming on a good day. But he had at least one repeat customer in the building, based on the friendly way he greeted Figg as "Lafcadio."

Tina told me cousin-to-cousin that she thought Palmer's eyewitness report might or might not be an example of an investigation going down a false trail, depending on how it turned out. What she didn't know was that the big finish was going to take place right in front of her, which was why Oscar and Gibbons were also on board this time around.

Palmer was followed backstage closely by Myles O'Rourke, looking about as pleased as the guest of honor at a cannibal picnic.

"You!" Palmer told him. "What are you doing here?"

"Good question," was the response.

"I invited him," Oscar said. He didn't make air quotes around "invited," but he didn't need to.

"Okay, so what's going on here?" Johanna said, whipping out a notebook—low-tech, yet functional. She was dressed for a day off in old jeans and a well-worn sweater, but that would never stop her from pursuing a good story. And a good story is what Mac had promised her, without details.

"The magician's trunk was stolen again," I informed her.

Tall Rawls looked at the trunk.

"But now it's back," I added.

She looked at me.

"Cool, isn't it?" Brian said.

Mac cleared his throat, a sound roughly resembling the roar of a freight train. "All that Jefferson said is true, and highly relevant to the murder at hand. This time the peregrinations of the Blackstone trunk were more than just distractions, as they were in the Pogue case. Rather, they were crucial to the killer of Tyler Garrett. And so was the theft of Mr. Garrett's video camera and the SD card it contained. I was—ahem—mistaken about that theft being a red herring to throw us off the trail. Chief Hummel here was right all along on that score. The murder was a robbery gone wrong, pure and not-so-simple."

I wish I had video of that rare example of Sebastian McCabe consuming humble pie, and Oscar practically popping his buttons with pride. But only after Mac had said this did Sam Phillips realize what was happening and pick up his camera to record the back-stage drama.

"So, who was the killer?" Tina blurted out.

As if Mac would make it that easy.

"As I indicated, a person who wanted the video," Mac said. "However, I only reached that conclusion reluctantly by process of elimination as I reconsidered the case yesterday in the privacy of my study." *Man cave.* "Was Mr. Garrett killed for what one might call 'romantic overreach'? That hardly seemed likely, based on Ms. Cody's description of his penchant for unwanted but less-than-physical advances. The next logical question, then, was, "What changed as a result of Mr. Garrett's death and the disappearance of his video camera?' A new videographer was sent to replace him. That was a notion that had promise."

"You're shitting me!" That came from behind the camera.

"Alas, even my fertile imagination as a fiction writer could not conceive of a reason why Mr. Phillips would wish for this assignment so much that he would kill for it. Especially since, as Ms. Cody told us, he had to fly in from just finishing another program in San Francisco.

"I was forced, therefore, to face the most likely scenario: Mr. Garrett's bludgeoning death was unintended and incidental to the real goal of the killer, which was to secure that video. For what purpose? Either to view it or to destroy it, most likely the latter.

"In speculating about motives, Jefferson quite logically offered the possibility that one of the Pogues or Belmonts had said something in an interview with Tina Cody that they later realized was harmful to them, and thus they needed to destroy the video. However—"

"You dismissed the idea because you didn't believe the theft of the camera was the key to the murder." That was Figg, trying to get himself some additional camera time on *Midwest Murders*.

"However, as I was about to say, Lafcadio, Ms. Cody and Mr. Garrett had not yet interviewed the Pogues before the Garrett murder, and Mr. Belmont had a solid alibi."

"Right," Tina said. "So, what was the killer after, if not one of my interviews?"

"And how did he even know whatever he wanted on the SD card existed?" Johanna asked.

"Interesting that you should be the one to ask," Mac said.

"Because Imogene Casey's page one photo in the *Observer* with your story showed what was in it," Lynda tossed in, working it backwards from the bottom line. She knew how this was going to end. "The person who became an accidental killer could see from that photo that Garrett videoed the contents of the trunk. And when it became clear from one of your later stories that Brian's finding of the trunk here at the theater would be re-enacted again for the *Midwest Murders* audience, it became necessary to grab the Blackstone trunk a second time so that the TV audience couldn't see what was in it."

Palmer eyed O'Rourke in a way that was almost comic in its obviousness.

"But then it showed up back here!" Johanna exclaimed, naturally confused.

"The trunk had to come back," Mac said, "because the killer could not be caught with it, nor could anyone be allowed to suspect that its contents led to the death of Tyler Garrett. Therefore, the killer—who was in this theater for Friday night's performance—set off the alarm and used the commotion as a cover for replacing the trunk. You really should do something about the lack of security here, Lafcadio."

"Wait a minute," Tina said before Figg could respond. "If the murderer killed Tyler for what was in the trunk, wouldn't it be obvious that the whatever-it-was was missing? I mean, you and anybody who looked inside knew what was in the trunk."

"In general, but not precisely." Mac nodded at Gibbons. On cue, the assistant chief opened the trunk to reveal a top hat, crystal ball, baseball cards, handcuffs, and a fake thumb (known in the trade as a thumb tip).

"It looks the same," Brian observed.

"That is exactly how the killer expected everyone to react—no perception of any change. However, 'you see but you do not observe,' in the words of Sherlock Holmes." Mac picked up the top baseball card. "This 1952 Ted Kluszewski #29 might be a welcome addition to the collection of a completist or a Cincinnati Reds fan, but my friend Kevin Carter assures me it cannot be worth more than a few hundred dollars in the best condition. I have no doubt the other cards here are of similar value. Kevin is equally certain that the card it replaced, the one clearly visible in this photo Jefferson took, is an entirely different story."

He held up his phone to display the photo I'd sent him on Saturday, one of the ones I took when Brian first found the trunk backstage in October. "This is what is known as a rookie card for a player named Willie Mays, who went on to have a superlative career. It was produced in 1951 by a now-defunct company called Bowman. The condition—and therefore the value—is difficult to tell from the photo, but Kevin assures me that it could sell for as much as half a million dollars. Though hardly in the same league as the $12.6 million paid at auction for a 1952 Mickey Mantle a year ago, which is a substantial amount even in these inflated times. And I am sure that Mr. Palmer knew the card's approximate value when Jefferson showed him the photo of it at his Balls & Strikes shop some weeks ago. Yet he pretended otherwise and said he would pay twenty-five hundred dollars for the entire lot. Do you wish to comment, Mr. Palmer?"

He didn't. But he looked like he'd been punched in the gut. Mac continued talking to him:

"It must have been a shock for you to see the front-page story in the *Observer*. If Tyler Garrett's video showing the contents of the trunk aired on *Midwest Murders* before I attempted to sell those baseball cards—and it might, given that I vowed not to do so until after the Belmont trial—someone viewing the program was likely to realize the true value of the Willie Mays card. Such a person could alert me, possibly even offering to buy it for hundreds of thousands of dollars before you could acquire it for a fraction of that. That is why you lured Tyler Garrett to the empty lot behind the Witch's Brew, hit him in the head, and took the revealing video."

Mac paused as if waiting for a reaction. He got none.

"How did he know you weren't going to sell the cards until after the trial?" Tina wondered.

"I mentioned that during a visit to his shop a couple of months ago," I admitted.[23]

"Go on," Tina told Mac.

"You must have been unnerved to realize that you had killed a man, Mr. Palmer, for that certainly was not your intention. I will give you that. But then, great sins like homicide are built on smaller sins like lying and stealing."

Actually, I'm pretty sure lying, stealing, and killing are all on that Top Ten list that begins "thou shalt not . . ."

"Your nerves must have already been strained to the breaking point when they received another jolt: The *Observer*

---

[23] See p. 105.

reported that a new videographer would be recording the re-enactment of the trunk finding all over again. Originally you intended to purchase the Willie Mays card from me at a price that would be considered a 'steal' in casual parlance. Now you would actually have to steal it and replace it with another card from your inventory that would arouse no reaction from anyone in the television audience informed about such matters. And to do that you had to both remove the trunk from my house and return it—this theater being a natural repository for it. Your industry would be admirable if it were not in service of despicable ends, Mr. Palmer."

This was no time for me to point out that Palmer, as a reader of my books, would have read in *Erin Go Bloody* about Mac's penchant for forgetting to set his burglar alarm.

"Is that it?" Palmer asked.

"There were a few other indicators," Mac told him. "For example, why would you go to the trouble of telling me there was a potential intruder at my home unless you knew about the theft that made his presence significant—a theft which was not a matter of public knowledge. And your own reported reason for being on the scene that night was rather weak; you scarcely needed to show up at my home in the evening to discuss a potential purchase from me that I had already indicated was months in the future."

"You asshole!" O'Rourke told Palmer.

"Finally," Mac rolled on, "there was the fact that your business did not seem very prosperous, by Jefferson's account, which could exacerbate your need for the money you could realize from selling the card."

The room was quiet for what seemed like minutes, but probably wasn't, as we all looked at Palmer. Finally, he said:

"I didn't hear anything about proof."

"Mac mentioned a baseball bat as the possible murder weapon, and you sell them in your shop," said Oscar, the Cincinnati Reds and Erin Eagles fan. "I think we'll find it there, or maybe in the dumpster outside. And no matter what you clean a surface with, blood can never be completely removed. We already have a search warrant, which we will execute today. If we get lucky, we might even find the burner phone you used to call Garrett, which you probably bought at Target earlier that day."

In some undefinable way, I read defeat in Ray Palmer's face at that moment as Oscar went on:

"Raymond Palmer, I am arresting you in connection with the murder of Tyler Garrett. You have the right to remain silent and refuse to answer questions. If you give up the right to remain silent, anything you say can and will be used against you in a court of law. You have the right to consult an attorney before speaking to the police and to have an attorney present during questioning now or in the future. If you cannot afford an attorney, one will be appointed for you before—"

"I'll need that," Palmer interrupted. "The public defender. I don't have the kind of money it will take to pay for a lawyer."

Chapter Ten
Cast Party

"Am I a bad person for liking the killer more than the victim?" I asked Lynda during pillow talk that night.

Her initial response was nonverbal and quite pleasant. Then she said, "You're not a bad person, Jeff Cody."

The *Midwest Murders* crew finished their work in Erin within a few more days, but Tina and her husband came back to town on Saturday, December 23, for the closing performance of *The Man Who Came to Dinner*. The final curtain was followed by a cast party in a private room at Bobbie McGee's, to which my cousin and cousin-in-law were invited.

By this time, the Ohio Bureau of Criminal Investigation, available to all police agencies in our state 24/7, had established that there was blood on a 1990 World Series bat at Balls & Strikes, and that the blood belonged to Tyler Garrett.

"I must say, luck was once again on your side in the murder of that video fellow," Lafcadio Figg told Mac while sucking oysters on the half-shell.

Mac raised an eyebrow. "How so?"

"Your logic was somewhat lacking in your analysis of who would have wanted the video. You completely overlooked the possibility that someone simply assumed, quite wrongly, that Ms. Cody and Mr. Garrett had recorded someone as saying something harmful to his or her interests."

"Such as who in regard to what, Lafcadio?"

"How should I know? You're the self-proclaimed sleuth!"

"Quite so! Even as you are the self-proclaimed impresario. Have you done anything to secure the backstage of the Lyceum so as to prevent a recurrence of objects reappearing there?"

And so forth.

"Are those two always like this?" Tina asked when Mac left to inspect the men's room.

"Always," Kate, Lynda, and I said together.

Ross Childress leaned across the table at me. "Your brother-in-law is like a fictional character."

"Not 'like,'" I corrected. "A fictional character is exactly what he is."

He looked at me like I'd had one too many brewskis.

"Mac created himself just as much as he created Damon Devlin," I explained, "and he's living the life that every other reader of whodunits can only fantasize about."

"Well, he's doing a damned good job of it."

I studied my Flying Pig Porter. Amidst all this bonhomie, I couldn't shake a certain melancholy. I decided to come out with it. "I still feel a little guilty about Garrett's murder. It wouldn't have happened if I hadn't shown Palmer the photos of the baseball cards in the trunk."

My spouse, my big sister, and my cousin made supportive noises.

"You can't think that way, T.J.," Kate instructed me. "That way madness lies."

And I've come to accept that she was right.

Speaking of madness, after delaying the process and keeping Roger Belmont out of court as long as she could, Erica Slade last week entered a plea of diminished responsibility. She contends her client committed murder under the influence of the fentanyl used to treat the pain he suffered from that electric scooter accident. Talk about chutzpah!

Meanwhile, SladeLaw's young associate Sally Fair has her hands full with an interesting twist of civil law: Septimus Pogue's insurance policy naming Clay Belmont as a beneficiary went upon Clay's death to Clay's estate—which means, essentially, Roger Belmont. The prosecutor is expected to argue that state law forbids Roger Belmont from profiting by his crime of killing Septimus Pogue—which he will do if the insurance money ultimately goes to him via the estate. That's why Roger killed Septimus, after all. But my sources tell me that Sally will argue that Clay Belmont, the immediate beneficiary, did nothing wrong and that Roger is entitled to inherit from him. My guess is that the biggest winner in that mess will be SladeLaw.

Phoebe Farleigh, of Farleigh & Farleigh, agreed to take on Ray Palmer as a client pro bono because she felt sorry for him, or maybe because she didn't mind taking her fee in baseball memorabilia. They quickly copped a plea to first-degree involuntary manslaughter and a 7-year prison sentence out of a possible 11 years. Shana Garrett, the victim's ex-wife, offered no objection.

In his sworn statement, Palmer said he never intended to sell the 1951 Willie Mays rookie card for hundreds of thousands of dollars. He just wanted the card. I'll never understand collectors.

A Few Words of Thanks

This is where I get to shout out to the members of Team Cody, those selfless souls who do the hard work of fixing all my errors of spelling, grammar, facts, and plot:

Ann Brauer Andriacco, for living with a writer;

Michael Andriacco, long-ago member of the magic duo Phantasm, who helped Jeff describe Magic Unlimited;

Peg Hausman, the consummate professional copyeditor and an old friend;

Marc Lehman, a professional magician who knows a trick or two;

Mike McSwiggin, for knowing how to kill a nursing home resident;

Jeff Suess, for his usual beta reading; and

Steve Winter, yet again, for giving the second draft a thorough reading and making suggestions that improved the text significantly.

Any errors that remain are mine, not theirs.

Special thanks, as always, to publisher Steve Emecz, who makes it possible for me to share these McCabe & Cody adventures with you. MX Publishing is a social enterprise venture that is both enterprising and venturesome.

About the Author

Dan Andriacco has been reading mysteries since he discovered Sherlock Holmes at the age of about nine and writing them almost as long. His first published work, however, was a Sherlock Holmes pastiche short story in 1990. The McCabe-Cody series began in 2011.

After almost 24 years as a reporter and business editor of a daily newspaper, Dan served as communications director for a religious non-profit for 20 years. He holds a master's degree in religion and a doctorate in ministry.

A Baker Street Irregular ("St. Saviour's, Near King's Cross"), Dan is editor of the BAKER STREET JOURNAL, Most Scandalous Member (leader) of the Tankerville Club of Cincinnati, and a member of numerous other scion societies of the BSI. He also wears bow ties. You can follow his long-running blog at www.danandriacco.com and his Facebook Fan Page, Dan Andriacco Mysteries.

Dan and his partner in criminous endeavors, Ann Brauer Andriacco, have three grown children and six grandchildren. They live in Cincinnati, Ohio, USA, about 40 miles downriver from the town Erin, which is located on no map.

Also from MX Publishing

Visit www.mxpublishing.com for dozens of other Sherlock Holmes novels, novellas, short story collections, Conan Doyle biographies, Holmes travel books, and more.

London-based MX Publishing is the award-winning, world's largest independent Sherlock Holmes Book publisher, with hundreds of books in print. Follow MX—

On Facebook:
https://www.facebook.com/BooksSherlockHolmes/

On Twitter
https://twitter.com/mxpublishing

On Instagram
https://www.instagram.com/mxpublishing/

www.ingramcontent.com/pod-product-compliance
Lightning Source LLC
Chambersburg PA
CBHW070900250626
47159CB00003B/1137